IN THE
SHADOW
OF WOLVES

ALVYDAS
ŠLEPIKAS

*Translated from the Lithuanian
by Romas Kinka*

ONEWORLD

A Oneworld Book

First published in North America, Great Britain and Australia by
Oneworld Publications, 2019
This paperback edition published 2020
Originally published in Lithuanian as *Mano vardas – Marytė* by
Lietuvos Rašytojų Sąjungos Leidykla, 2011

ISBN 978-1-78607-704-2
ISBN 978-1-78607-469-0 (eBook)

The translation of this book was supported by the Lithuanian Culture Institute

Printed and bound in Great Britain by Clays Ltd, Elcograf S.p.A.

Oneworld Publications
10 Bloomsbury Street, London WC1B 3SR, England
3754 Pleasant Ave, Suite 100, Minneapolis, MN 55409, USA

Stay up to date with the latest books,
special offers, and exclusive content from
Oneworld with our newsletter

Sign up on our website
oneworld-publications.com

Named a Book of the Year by *The Times*, 2019

'T... ...trait of a forgotten tragedy is ...'
The Times

'Has the simple narrative structure and heightened quality of a fable... Šlepikas has a vivid vision and lyricism which lifts the prose and ensures it is anything but derivative.'
Big Issue

'A heartbreaking blend of historical facts and literary prose.'
Foreword Reviews

'This is stunning. Cinematic, powerful... [*In the Shadow of Wolves*] has an irresistible, emotional pull that is as fascinating as it is brilliant, with a sense of heartbreak rather than trauma.'
Victoria's Book Reviews

'A raw and tender true tale... It's no wonder that this elegant and intricate debut has garnered its Lithuanian author many awards.'
LoveReading

'Vivid, highly dramatic and compelling... Alvydas Šlepikas has broken the dam of silence.'
Dresdner Neueste Nachrichten

'*In the Shadow of Wolves*...reminded me in some ways of reading the work of Cormac McCarthy... Šlepikas imbues barren East Germany and the forests of post-war Lithuania with the dark undertones of a fairytale.'
Splice

'This novel finds the perfect balance between documentary and literary narrative.'
Kieler Nachrichten

The author is grateful to
Mrs Renate, Rolandas, Ričardas,
his mother Renata, Evaldas and Rita
for their support and help in writing this book.

In memory of
Almantas Grikevičius

EVERYTHING RISES UP *from the past as if through fog. People and events are enveloped in the snow carried on the wind and the mist that hovers in the silence. All is distant but not forgotten. Some details are clear, others are already lost, as in a faded photograph. Time and forgetfulness have covered everything in snow and sand, in blood and murky water.*

People appear as if emerging through a mist, a snowstorm, a winter fog; they grow dark, casting a shadow on the trampled, blood-soaked earth, and then are gone. Individual episodes surface for one brief flash of memory, or as a few marks on the dotted line of history, scattered in no particular order:

here are the Russian words on a poster seen on reaching the other side of the Nemunas river*: 'Soldier of the Red Army! Before you lies the lair of the fascist beast';

here are the Russian soldiers laden with their plunder – clocks, curtains, silver dishes;

here is a woman's headless body nailed to a wall;

here is a crowd of starving people tearing apart the fallen corpse of a water carrier's nag;

here is a mother with her children walking straight into the Nemunas rumbling with ice floes, disappearing into the river

---

*   The Nemunas is Lithuania's largest river, rising in Belarus and flowing through Lithuania before draining into the Couronian Lagoon and then into the Baltic Sea at Klaipėda. In places it also marks the border between Lithuania and the Russian exclave of Kaliningrad. The territory formerly known as East Prussia has been called Kaliningrad since its occupation by the Soviet Union in 1945, when all German inhabitants who had not yet fled west were forcibly removed and the region subsequently colonised by citizens from the Soviet Union.

1

without a word, without a single thought in her head, as if drowning oneself were a simple, everyday act;

here are corpses brought up by the river, blackened and swollen, without first names, without surnames;

here are graves dug up;

here are the ruins of bombed churches;

here are Russian pamphlets handed out to Soviet soldiers, urging them: 'Kill all the Germans, their children too. There are no innocent Germans. Take their possessions, take their women. That is your right, those are the spoils of war';

here are mothers bartering, selling some of their children to Lithuanian farmers for potatoes, flour and food, so that their other children can survive;

here are soldiers, drunk and laughing, shooting birds for fun, and then shooting people just as merrily and mindlessly, without thinking – the fire of war has hardened them, like clay in blast furnaces;

here are women digging trenches, dying from hunger and fatigue;

here are children setting off shells left behind by the war;

here are wolves that have grown accustomed to eating human flesh;

here is a dog with a blackened human hand in its teeth;

here are the eyes of the starving, here is famine, famine and famine;

here are corpses – death and corpses;

here are the new arrivals, colonists, destroying everything that has survived – churches, castles, cemeteries, drainage systems, animal pens;

here are the empty and desolate fields, in which even the wind loses its way, not finding a single familiar path among the ruins and barren wastes;

here is postwar Prussia, trampled underfoot, raped, stood against a wall and shot.

FRAGMENTS OF THE past flickered and vanished, emerging from the darkness as if they were a shadow-play, like a black-and-white film.

It was the winter of 1946.

A cold and terrible postwar winter, a time of desolation. A bridge suspended between heaven and earth across the Nemunas. The wind carried a dusting of snow along the river as if it were a highway. In places there was ice, off-white like marble. It was cold, at least minus 20 degrees Celsius.

There were metal struts criss-crossing each other like an opaque net. The wind whistled through them. The bridge howled the songs of storms.

A soldier's own strange song drifted along on the wind from the east.

Through the metal struts you could see dark figures moving on the other side of the river.

Pasted on the bridge there were posters, signs and newspapers proclaiming victory, encouraging the soldiers to show no mercy, to kill, and warning that access was allowed only with a permit from the military authorities.

The edge of one of the posters was ragged and fluttered in the wind. The song of longing grew louder.

On the bridge were two guards: a singing Asian and a Russian. The Russian was trying to light a roll-up but the wind kept putting out his match, and this made him angry. The narrow-eyed soldier's singing irritated him too.

The black dots across the river were drawing closer – they were German children trying to cross the frozen Nemunas. There were about seven of them.

The Russian couldn't stand it any longer.

'For fuck's sake shut your mouth, you idiot.'

The Asian smiled. He was quiet for a while, and then said, under his breath: 'Idiot, idiot, you're the idiot.'

The wind was whistling, the motherland was far away, the roll-up fell apart, the match broke in the soldier's calloused hands.

The Asian laughed: 'Hey, Ivan...'

'My name's not Ivan, it's Yevgeny. They call me Zhenya.'

'Look, Ivan, the little Germans are running.'

The German children were running across the ice like partridges. A couple of the smaller children lagged behind a little.

The Russian soldier shouted: 'Stop! Go back! Stop! That's an order! Stop, you fascist pigs!'

But the bridge was high up, the wind masked the guard's voice and they ran on. They could see a person on the bridge waving his arms about, but they couldn't understand the soldier's language.

'Hey, Ivan.'

'My name's not Ivan, you idiot.'

'They're telling you to suck their dicks, Ivan...'

'I'm going to kill you.'

'Calm down, you fool.'

The Russian took a grenade, pulled the pin out and threw it at the group of children. Both soldiers crouched down to avoid the shrapnel, and the blast reverberated like a thunderclap in the icy air.

The smoke cleared.

One of the children had fallen through the ice and was struggling to climb out. It was cold and an icy mist rose from the water. The other children were running back, running away from death.

The noise died down, and for a moment there was complete silence. Then a strange sound like the wail of a dying beast cut through the silence, high-pitched and endless. Another child was badly injured. He lay writhing, his feet kicking out at the ice; the scream was coming from him. As he twisted and turned, blood seeped out from under him, painting an ever-larger area of snow and ice: a stain of colour in a black world.

A six-year-old boy, scared to death, stood between the one who was injured and the one who was trying to get out of the hole in the ice. It was as if he'd turned to stone. He had no control over his legs; the screeching pierced his body. His eyes were filled with horror.

It was little Hansel – we'll get to know him later.

The Asian raised his rifle, took aim and fired. The screaming stopped; the injured child was no longer moving. Hansel woke from his stupor and started to run, shouting something. He wasn't running towards the shore but along the frozen river. A couple of shots followed, but Hansel ran on.

Having missed him, the Asian soldier shook his head.

The other child was still trying to get out of the hole in the ice, using every ounce of his strength.

The Russian soldier spat and looked down at the little child below him in the river. They were hardly struggling any more.

The child's head went under. One hand was still holding on to the ice, until finally it too disappeared.

The Russian soldier at last managed to light his roll-up.

The wind was whistling.

Again a sad, wild song was heard.

NIGHT WAS DRAWING in. It came so quickly in winter. To Eva it seemed that for the last few months it had always been night. The never-ending winter, the never-ending snow-storms, frosts, twilight, cold, wind, the never-ending hunger. The cold passed through her clothes to her very heart, to her bones and her brain. Eva began to feel dizzy from hunger again; it had been a long time since she had last eaten. Whenever she managed to find a morsel of something she gave it to the children. The world was turning on its axis and for a moment darkness covered her eyes, but her friend Martha, who never gave in, grabbed her by the elbow. 'Hold on,' she said, 'hold on, Eva, remember the children.' Eva didn't need reminding; the children were the only thing she thought about – Monika, Renate, pampered Helmut, who was so gentle but weak, sickly, so different from her Heinz. *Where is he now, my Heinz, my little boy? He set off for Lithuania by train almost a week ago. Is he alive, is he healthy, what is he eating, does he have anywhere to rest his head?*

People stood motionless, hunched up against the wind and the cold, pressing close to one another like sheep – dark silhouettes in the gloom of the approaching night, in the grip of the dying day. Eva leant against Martha. It was good that there was someone next to her who was stronger and tougher. Martha always knew the way out of any situation. Eva didn't think she'd ever seen her friend cry. Even now, when all the days were but one big, black day of loss, one big hole in the ground dug for a grave. No, Martha had never cried. She believed in life. Even now she was a pillar, a shelter for Eva, who was afraid of everything and easily frightened.

6

Oh, Martha, Martha, how good to have you by my side, how good it is that you are by my side, only I can't tell you that, it's impossible to say the words. If there were no more Martha the world would be without compass – though now it was more a formless mass than a world.

Finally two soldiers showed up: two youths, probably only eighteen, but stern, serious. They were dragging along a huge pot with scraps of food in it, mostly potato peels, the potato peels the crowd had been so desperately waiting for. The people – the elderly, women and children, Eva and Martha among them – instantly came to life. Their eyes seemed to catch fire and everyone moved forward; they were all starving, tired of waiting, freezing, their faces drawn, their bodies swathed in rags. Everyone gathered round, but they knew they had to wait for the command, for permission. The young soldiers shouted something, but Eva didn't speak Russian; all she knew was 'thank you' and 'goodbye', and now she'd also learnt to say 'bread' and 'potatoes'. But the young soldiers didn't say 'bread' and they didn't say 'thank you'. They were shouting: 'What are you doing, you spawn of the devil? What are you doing, you fascists? Get back or you'll get a beating! Don't climb over each other!' No one was climbing over anyone, all they were doing was hesitantly moving closer; everyone was ready to snatch their portion, which would be as large as they could manage to grab. Eva and the others approached the young soldiers, the pot full of leftover scraps and potato peels. For a moment the space around her seemed to distort, people's hands and faces lost their contours, everything expanded and then shrank again, everything slowed down. The soldiers emptied the pot straight out onto the ground, right there by the army canteen at the end of the yard. Once there had been a tavern here, now it was a canteen. They were throwing out a lot today; they weren't always so lucky, especially in the evenings.

The young soldier shouted: 'Here you are, help yourselves, you fascists!' The only thing he said in German was 'here you are', everything else was in Russian, but to the starving, hungry and deathly cold people, whatever he might or might not have said wasn't important. They rushed towards the potato peels and the other scraps, grabbed them and stuffed them into little linen sacks and bags. An old woman began to yell: 'That's mine, that's mine! I want to live too!' She fell, someone tripped over her and stepped on her hand, making her yell again. Eva went to pieces; she stopped for a moment, perhaps half a second, suddenly seeing herself as a worm wriggling around in the leftovers, but the image was immediately dispelled by Martha's voice, saying: *Remember the children.* Or perhaps it wasn't Martha at all, perhaps it was her own voice reminding her of the children, her inner maternal voice. Like a predator she grabbed, tore, pulled and stuffed the frozen potato peels into her little linen sack. She was probably crying too. Or perhaps it was only a few tears from the cold and the wind.

'Pigs is what they are, they're not even human,' said the soldier in Russian, tapping a woman's cigarette holder against the corner of the building to get rid of the bits of tobacco in it.

A snowstorm was raging.

The strong wind whipped the falling snow into people's eyes. Eva and Martha were hurrying, but it was hard to walk; the silhouettes of their bodies, bent forward, began to disappear into the falling night. Finally they reached the former dairy, then the wool-carding workshop, its corner destroyed by an artillery shell. The building had been opened up like the flank of a slaughtered animal, but inside there was only bottomless darkness. These buildings, so devoid of life, petrified her; she was always seeing shadows persecuting her and Martha. She was sweating, though the cold was going right through her. In this snowstorm the little town where she was born now seemed alien – horrible and malignant.

A shot echoed somewhere. Then another. The women quickened their pace. The sound of a Russian accordion came in waves through the howling of the storm and the swirling snow. Even though it was a foreign sound, it had a calming effect because it was so unexpected, as if from another world. It even appeared to Eva that she herself, her consciousness, was playing this music, this simple, wild music in a major key. Eva held on tightly to the potato peels she'd grabbed by the soldiers' canteen. At home the children were waiting, hungry, her children who were dearer to her than life itself. Eva would have liked to howl like a she-wolf; she would have liked to cut off a piece of her own body and feed those hungry children, innocent, suffering children punished by God. She would bring back the scraps thrown out by the Russian soldiers, and her sister-in-law Lotte would dry the potato peels on a metal camping stove, then grind them into flour in an old coffee mill to bake flat bread. Eva wouldn't have known how to survive without Lotte. And Martha.

Eva and Martha were hurrying home, hunched up against the wind and the fear that someone might speak to them. From time to time, light broke through the falling snow; they could just about make out vehicles, soldiers, shapes of some kind. Someone was laughing, someone shouted at them, but the women pretended they didn't hear. It was important not to stop, not to turn around, to pass by quietly. Eva strode out and measured every step with a syllable from the prayer taught by Jesus: 'Our Father, who art in heaven, hallowed be thy name...' She had never been religious – more of a free thinker – but now she repeated that prayer over and over again, and had even taught it to the children. It seemed to her that it helped, that the saints helped, those words that had come from the lips of God. Martha made fun of her: 'You've become a religious old biddy.' Eva wasn't angry with Martha. It was impossible to be angry with her – with this beautiful, sturdy woman who couldn't be broken by any misfortune; you couldn't be angry with her, not with that infectious laugh of hers. It was hard to believe, but even now Martha laughed from time to time. Perhaps in an attempt to lighten the mood.

Suddenly someone seized Eva by the arm. 'Babushki, babushki,' a drunk soldier shouted and laughed, his eyes like those of a madman. Eva was so shocked that she screamed. She pushed the soldier, but he had a firm grip on her and they both fell over. Eva smelt a strong odour of alcohol coming from the soldier's mouth; she pushed, kicked, scrambled up. The soldier kept his hold on her sleeve, but Martha helped and pulled him off Eva. Other men had gathered around them now, laughing with bared teeth.

The soldiers rushed towards them, materialising from the blinding snow. They were all shouting something, laughing; it seemed they were egging one another on, speaking German now: 'Ladies, don't be afraid, we're very gentle.' Then laughter.

Martha broke free from another attacker and someone grabbed Eva by her leg. One of the other soldiers had fallen down, but even on the ground he was hungry for a woman.

Finally, they both managed to escape. They ran as fast as they could, but their attackers were not about to give up so easily. They gave chase and someone fired a shot into the air. Eva pressed the food she was carrying for the children to her breast; she simply wasn't going to give up her treasure. The women turned off the path, diving into the darkness between the buildings – they knew, or had once known, everything, every inch of this small town. They raced past the school, then the burnt-out shell of the police station, the yards, the gardens. The most important thing was to lose the attackers, to lead them astray in the snowstorm, otherwise they might follow them home; after all, they weren't going to be stopped by the woodshed's flimsy locks. Eva's family were living in their old woodshed, where the new arrivals – a concussed officer and his woman – had moved them as soon as they'd taken over their house. The woodshed was their home now.

Eva didn't have enough energy to run any more; she found shelter behind the wall of a building, crouched down and squeezed into a corner, and waited. Where was Martha? Where could she have disappeared to? They had been running together, they had both managed to defend themselves, to break away from their drunken attackers, but where was she now? Suddenly Eva heard screams, and a couple of shots being fired. *Oh Lord, protect me and my friend Martha, protect her family, her children and my children, lead us out of this valley of death, return our lives to us.*

Eva tried to walk on, but was caught on a branch.

No, it wasn't a branch. It was an arm.

It was a frozen corpse. The roads were lined with them, and people were saying that wolves had grown used to eating human flesh. But why all this talk about wolves when the people themselves had become wolves?

Eva wasn't surprised, she wasn't shocked by this dead being, only a little startled.

She listened to the night and the wind, made sure that there was no one around and sensed her way home. Her figure vanished into the night.

The corpse stayed behind, its hand outstretched, imploring.

It no longer felt the cold.

THE COLD. IT found its way through every gap, especially in a woodshed unfit for human habitation. The sound of the raging, moaning snowstorm penetrated the thin walls. There was a paraffin candle on a box that served as a table, which had burnt down almost to a stub. Luckily Auntie Lotte had managed to collect enough of them. She had never believed in victory, or in crowds of people with raised hands, screaming in ecstasy, waiting for their beloved Führer, stamping the ground to the rhythm of stirring marches – *do you remember how, in Berlin, we were all entranced, shouting: 'Deutschland! Deutschland! Deutschland!'? How both the old and the young women were ready to open their wombs to the leader's seed?* But not Auntie Lotte – no, she was a writer, and once upon a time she had written books. Where were those books now? Who needed them now, who needed them when the only things that existed were the wind and the cold, death and starvation? The candle's flame fluttered in the wind. The storm was howling, licking the wooden walls of their living quarters. Inside it was always cold, only the metal stove helped a little; you had to keep it going all the time, the firewood had to be brought in from outside, collected in the town. It was the children's job to do this, but they were all so weak from hunger that every trip into town was now a challenge. Even more so because of the soldiers, and the new colonists there – mostly injured, traumatised, shell-shocked officers who had been left behind. They'd been allotted houses, they'd been told to take what they wanted, without a thought being given to those already living in them. Every building, every house, every yard had an owner. *Take everything, that's your right, those are the spoils of war.* An officer and his bawling wife were now living in their house. The man had trouble using his right arm, but still managed to beat his wife. The first time they'd heard the screams of that plump woman who wore Eva's nightgown as a dress, everyone was scared. It sounded like he was going to kill her. Although death was all around them, it was a horrible thought. A man beating his own wife was quite a strange thing, especially when you were six years old, like Renate, or five, like Helmut. But he didn't kill her then, or any of the other times. In the beginning they were scared whenever they heard the unusual, loud lament that continued through the night, seemingly coming from the most unhappy person in the world, or perhaps some wild animal. But after a while it was no longer alarming – to them, it became a kind of love song.

When the first Russian soldiers appeared, people prayed. They were afraid, but they believed that the descendants of Tolstoy and Dostoyevsky would not be cruel and savage conquerors. A neighbour would come into their yard to smoke a pipe, and would say to their grandfather that the Russians were educated people, there was nothing to be afraid of, they were human beings like everyone else. But then the Russians showed up, and some were quite short, the rifles slung over their shoulders, banging against their heels, and it was difficult to see how their feet didn't get tangled up in their long greatcoats. The neighbour soon became convinced that these lads, on whose faces the war had left its mark, had never read Tolstoy, that they had read something else, had experienced something else. That for them, hardened as they were by several of the most brutal years of war, one more death was of no great importance, and besides, they were consumed by their desire for revenge. The neighbour, who could mumble the odd word of Russian, tried to speak to them, but soon he was hanging from a branch of the apple tree in his own yard, his feet unable to reach the ground. Their grandfather protested against the fact that his family was being turned out of their house, out of their beloved farmstead, and left only with the woodshed in the yard, in which he and his son's five children, his daughter and his daughter-in-law would have to find shelter. He went off to look for justice from the victors' leaders, and never came back. Auntie Lotte, his daughter, had told him: 'Papa, don't go, you won't change anything, you won't—' But he, despite being old and ill, was a veteran of the First World War, and proud. He put his tobacco pouch in his pocket, and took some expensive items – gold and silver spoons, a cigar case with an eagle on it, and some other small things that might be able to save their family, their house, their home. After all, their children needed warmth, and beds to sleep in. 'We'll give away everything if it can save our home,' said Grandfather, but never returned. And so the woodshed became their home.

True, they weren't turned out immediately.

The first conquerors had seemed better. Eva liked playing music. She had even studied at the conservatoire, but hadn't graduated because she had fallen in love with a tall, constantly smiling, freckled farmer by the name of Rudolph. He took her back to his farm in East Prussia. At first it was hard for this young lady from Berlin, but love conquers all – child after child was born. Rudolph bought her a wonderful upright piano. She had wanted a grand, but that would have been too expensive for a farmer's family. Then the war began, and Rudolph said his goodbyes. Eva played Mozart and Rachmaninov, and sang those folk songs the children liked. Oh, that was a blessed, happy time, something that had probably never existed, something that she had probably only dreamt about in the cold woodshed, sleeping the sleep of the hungry.

The first arrivals were more cultured. When a Russian captain found out there was a piano in their house, he would come round, make his apologies, ask Eva's permission and sit down at the instrument. He played wonderfully; most probably he had been a musician before the war. His name was Andrei.

He usually played Beethoven. He liked the 'Moonlight Sonata' most of all, with its very dramatic ending, and to Eva it seemed that it wasn't her piano being played, but a fine concert grand. One day, Captain Andrei opened some sheet music of her mother's that was lying next to it. The pieces were unfamiliar to him; they were compositions by Erik Satie. Eva didn't tell him where she'd got it from. Rudolph had served in occupied Paris and sent it to her. The music, seemingly so simple, yet captivating, was Eva's favourite. It wasn't clear whether it was Satie she loved, or the fact that her beloved Rudolph himself had sent it to her. Perhaps both. Andrei began to play Satie too, and particularly liked *Gnossienne* No. 5. Little Renate also adored it, and would dance to it in the kitchen as the Russian captain played.

Then the captain left, and others came who had no need of the piano, nor of Satie and Beethoven. They confiscated everything, drove out the household pets, and banished the family to the woodshed. Grandfather never returned. No one tried to talk about him any more. He had left, and that was a fact.

There was no piano in the woodshed; there was almost nothing there, only the metal stove they had managed to get by some miracle and which they relied on every day, the candles obtained by Auntie Lotte from who knows where, and the few things they had managed to carry out of the house: some clothes, bedding and Grandfather's sheepskin coat. Instead of a bed they had planks, on which Renate, Monika, Brigitte and Helmut were now lying covered with everything they had, or almost everything. Auntie Lotte was sitting next to them, stoking the stove and giving them a fairy tale instead of food. Pinned to the walls were the photographs they'd managed to save in which a camera had frozen happy moments from the past. The whole family was pictured: Grandfather, their father Rudolph, a smiling Heinz and their smiling mother Eva, and everyone, everyone was smiling, laughing, full of happiness and contentment. Lotte's glance slid along the walls like an X-ray, scanning the smiles in the photographs. She sighed and threw some scraps of wood into the stove. It would have been better if the children had fallen asleep, but they were awake. They were waiting for Auntie Lotte to continue the tale. She was always telling them stories, unsuccessfully trying to distract them from their hunger and the cold. The cold was everywhere, it was in the blood. Hunger was gnawing at them from the inside like an icy fire that could not be assuaged; it was smouldering – it would probably never die out. The children could no longer remember a time when they hadn't been hungry. And whatever fairy tale they were being told, there was always some mention of bread, of meat, of turnips, of delicious food.

Eva still hadn't come back. A snowstorm was howling and whistling outside, interspersed with gunshots. Somewhere, dogs were tearing into each other.

'When's Mama coming home?' asked Renate.

'She's coming, she's coming.'

In the night, Hansel secretly got up and crept outside so his stepmother wouldn't hear him. The moon was high, its light playing on the road, the stones shining like buttons. Hansel decided to fill his pockets with those moon buttons. He filled his pockets with the shining stones and went back to bed. When dawn broke, the stepmother came in to wake the children: 'Get up, lazybones, we're going to cut down some trees, we've run out of firewood.'

'When's Mama coming home?' asked Helmut.

'She'll be home, she'll be home soon…be patient.'

And they all went into the forest. Gretel was walking along, silently crying, thinking about what was going to happen next – *Stepmother will set us on the wrong path through the forest* – but Hansel was striding out boldly; he seemed cheerful and happy. Every few steps he dropped some of the stones he'd collected in the night. The father told the children to gather twigs and build a bonfire. The children built the bonfire and their father lit it. 'Now,' said their stepmother, 'you rest by the fire. Your father and I will go and cut some firewood. But,' she said, 'don't move away from the bonfire, because the forest animals may tear you to pieces.'

'When's Mama coming home?' asked Monika.

'She's coming, Monika dear, she's coming.'

The stepmother and father left the children by the bonfire and went deeper into the forest. They hadn't gone to cut firewood. All they had done was tie a log to a tree: the log swayed in the wind, and when it hit the tree it sounded like the blows from an axe. The children were very hungry. They hadn't had so much as a crumb of bread to eat for a long time, but they knew that sleep could conquer hunger – you fell asleep, and you no longer wanted to eat. And so they fell asleep and they slept peacefully by the fire that kept them warm, right until midnight.

'I want to eat... I want to eat,' Helmut began to sob.

'Mama's going to be back soon, she'll bring something, just be patient.'

'I want to eat.'

'Listen to the fairy tale until Mama brings back something to eat. Get some sleep.'

'I don't want the fairy tale, I want some bread!'

Brigitte, his older sister, couldn't stand Helmut's constant moaning any more:

'Go to sleep, stop snivelling! You think it's worse for you than for us? You think you're hungrier than we are? Helmut, we all want to eat, but you have to be patient. Tomorrow we're all going to go and look for bread and we'll find some, we will find some. And perhaps your brother Heinz will come back from Lithuania and bring back all kinds of things. Sleep now, sleep, my little child.'

'And what if a wolf's eaten Heinz in the forest?'

Lotte poured some boiled water from the teapot into a cup, and gave it to Helmut. There hadn't been any wolves around for a long time; these days they existed only in fairy tales. People were like wolves now.

'Drink the hot water, it'll warm you up, you'll sleep better if your tummy is warm.'

Helmut drank.

The other children also asked for some hot water.

During the winter it was dark, but never completely dark, the snow driving back the coming night with its whiteness. Eva was hurrying. She slipped, fell, got up, stopped, and listened to see if anyone was following her, if she could hear any shouting or gunshots. The snowstorm and the night's dim light made it difficult to get her bearings, but she knew that the strip of light above the rooftops marked where the Russian army headquarters were, in the former school building. It meant that she now had to turn left. Between the houses there would be a narrow passage, and Eva would then find herself in the town's main street; she only had to cross it and would be almost home.

The swirling snow was making her eyelids stick together. Eva clasped the linen sack with the potato peels to her breast – she needed to be at home, to get home as quickly as possible. She turned a corner and happened on some Russian soldiers, smoking. For a moment Eva didn't know what to do, but then she started running, diving into the darkness, running as fast as she could, catching her breath between the houses. The soldiers had noticed her, and she turned right so that her footprints would lead them in the wrong direction. They were shouting something in Russian, whistling, perhaps swearing, perhaps they were simply surprised: 'Look, a woman – a German, not at all bad – where are you running, you bitch – where're you running to? – we're not going to do anything bad to you – you'll see how much you're going to like it – hey, woman, stop, stop!'

Eva was already very close to her yard, very close to her children. She was standing with her back to the barn, listening, but her heart was beating so loudly, thumping so loudly that she couldn't hear anything. Eva was terrified, she was cold, despair slowly began to overwhelm her. How long would she be able to stand here? How long would she be able to hide, when the raging wind was going right through her from all directions, and her cheeks, which had already lost all feeling, were now frozen after she'd spent so long being lost in the night, running from her persecutors?

Auntie Lotte was telling the tale of Hansel and Gretel, she was telling them about how Hansel dropped breadcrumbs on the path so they wouldn't get lost.

'I wouldn't drop any breadcrumbs,' said Helmut, 'I'd eat them. Grandfather used to spread honey on a large slice of bread, but I didn't want to eat it, and Grandfather said the day would come when, after a shit, I'd want to eat but there'd be nothing to eat.'

'Don't use words like that,' said Auntie Lotte.

'How did he know?' asked Helmut. 'How did he know, Auntie Lotte, the day would come when we'd be as hungry as we are now and want to eat?'

'Shut your mouth!' shouted Brigitte. 'Shut your mouth! We all want to eat, why are you the only one whining and whinging, why are you the only one who can't calm down? You've been told Mama will come home, she'll bring something. Go to sleep, otherwise I won't be able to stop myself, I'll pull your ear off, you'll see how angry I'll be!'

'Children, children, don't fight, don't quarrel, shh! Try to sleep. We can't be angry with each other now, we have to be nice to each other, we have to help each other, it's the only way. It's the only way we'll survive, only by helping each other.'

'Shh! Can you hear that?' asked Renate. Everyone listened.

Yes, there were footsteps, quick steps, the crunching of snow, yes, it couldn't be a mistake, it was Mama, she'd come back! Auntie Lotte went to the door and asked: 'Who is it?'

'Lotte, it's me,' Eva's muffled voice could be heard from the other side. Lotte opened the door. Eva came inside, bringing with her a gust of snow. Lotte quickly closed the door. Eva collapsed by the iron stove. She said: 'Lotte, I've brought something.'

'What is it, what happened to you, Eva?' Lotte quietly asked her.

'I was being chased, they were chasing me, I don't know if I managed to get away from them. Soldiers were chasing us, Martha and I became separated.'

'Didn't I tell you, didn't I say you shouldn't be walking around the town like that? Come here, put this on your face.'

Lotte had grabbed some ashes and dirt, and began to put them on Eva's face, hands, clothes and neck, but especially on her face.

'I told you to be careful, to hide yourself! You have to put some shit on you, you have to smell, to look like a witch, and never, ever look them in the eye.'

Renate was watching, she saw how dirty her mother was beginning to look. She started laughing. 'Mama is going to look like an old witch!'

Blow out the candle, blow out the candle, light is spilling out through the small glass window, through the smallest cracks.

But it was already too late.

Someone was banging on the door, kicking it. Everyone huddled together. Eva pressed herself against a wall, and the children formed a ball on the makeshift bed, holding each other.

Lotte opened the door. A trio of soldiers barged in. A blinding light dispelled the darkness: one of the intruders had a powerful torch, a war trophy.

'Well, how are you getting on, you fascists? All good? Why are you sitting in the dark? Are you trying to hide?'

The torchlight was dancing around the woodshed, highlighting the frightened faces. The spot of light came to a rest on Eva's face.

'Look at these Germans, they're horrible animals, half-wild! Why can't they wash? Look at this stinking scarecrow!'

One of the soldiers kicked Eva in the side and laughed. Another one pulled the blanket off the frightened children, huddled together and holding on to each other tightly. Helmut began to squeal and squeak like a beaten animal.

Lotte dropped down at the soldier's feet, seized him by the hands, kissed them, and begged him in her broken Russian: 'Don't touch the children, don't touch the children, for God's sake!'

The soldier laughed. 'You see, bitch, how quickly you've learnt Russian!'

He pushed Auntie Lotte away with his foot, and one of the other soldiers pulled the screaming Helmut away. 'Shut your mouth, you little rat!' He threw him on the bed, gripped Brigitte's arm, tore Monika and Renate's hands off her, and yanked the girl off the bed. Everyone rushed to defend Brigitte, crying and begging, even Helmut grabbed the soldier's boot, shouting the only Russian word he knew: 'Spasibo, spasibo, spasibo!'

Auntie Lotte was almost hanging from the soldier's arm. He threw her off, lifted his rifle and hit her on the head with the heavy butt. She collapsed, and lay on her back as if dead.

The children began to scream even more; they were cry-ing, imploring the soldiers. Eva could hardly breathe, she was holding on to Brigitte, her arms around her – *kill me, kill me*; her head was swimming from hunger and despair, images began to merge and swim before her eyes.

No one had noticed that once again there was a candle burning in the woodshed. The third soldier was survey-ing their modest dwelling, looking at the photographs on the walls. He smiled as if he'd remembered something, lit a cigarette, twirled his thick moustache with a thumb and forefinger, and then turned around to see what was going on, as if only now aware of the screams and the pleading. His face was old, wrinkled, tired. He was battle-hardened. He had witnessed the death and trauma of his friends, seen thousands of corpses, lain in trenches in his own blood, hopeless, almost entirely covered by earth. Loudly, clearly, in an authoritative voice, he said: 'Leave her alone.' But no one heard him, so he grabbed the soldier who had taken hold of Brigitte by the shoulders and shook him: 'Let her go.'

'Why?' asked the soldier. 'Why should I let her go, this German?'

'She's still a girl, she's a child,' said the old soldier. 'Remember your sister, Vanya.'

'They should all be butchered, this fascist scum,' screamed Vanya, 'or they'll grow up and breed more fascists!'

'We're human beings! We're human beings!' the old man shouted right into the soldier's ear.

For a moment they stared at each other, angry and men-acing. But then Vanya let go of the girl.

All he did then was kick the kettle that was boiling on the metal stove, look at the frightened family and go out. The second soldier followed him.

The elderly soldier stayed behind and spoke. In German. 'Daub some shit on her as well. She'll soon be a woman.'

'Spasibo, spasibo,' whispered Lotte, 'spasibo.'

The soldier left, and they ran over to Auntie Lotte. Blood was slowly trickling from her head, and one of her eyes was swollen.

They hugged each other.

'Everything's fine…children…your mama's brought back some food…I'm going to make you something to eat,' said Auntie Lotte.

Dawn was breaking. A train rattled by in the distance.

The children had fallen asleep. Lotte was also sleeping. Eva was sitting alone by the stove, staring in front of her, thinking of nothing. She opened the door of the stove and threw in some more firewood. The fire had a calming effect, its flame was comforting. Eva remembered Rudolph, she remembered her parents, all her nearest and dearest whom she hadn't seen for so long, and who perhaps were no longer in the land of the living. She suddenly wanted to see their eyes, their faces, their smiles. She lit the candle and, carefully, so as not to wake the others, pulled out a small wooden box from under the bed and opened it – this is where the letters were; she laid them out in order and smelt them. They smelt of peace and the past, or perhaps it only seemed that way, *perhaps I'm being naive*, thought Eva. She took out several photographs, one of which showed her husband in military uniform. He looked so manly, so handsome – *where are you now, what sort of place are you living in, what are you eating, what songs are you listening to, are you alive, do you remember us?* She couldn't believe that this person, her beloved, the father of her children, might for a long time already have been lying by some wayside; she didn't even want to think about that. He had to be alive, they would find one another – why shouldn't they find one another, why should he have perished? After all, throughout history people have gone to war, but they've also come back. It doesn't matter if they return as the defeated…

Eva was looking at the photograph, then at Helmut sleeping, at the girls, at Lotte; forgetting herself, she smiled. She heard another train rattling by in the distance.

Night was retreating, the snowstorm slowly dying down – soon it would be light.

Through the snowstorm, which seemed to be stretching itself out before the dawn, through the whirling gusts of snow, a tiny figure could be seen coming from the direction of the railroad tracks. It was Heinz. He was returning from Lithuania, carrying a canvas sack on his back.

The boy was hurrying, though he was very tired.

The small, lonely traveller disappeared into the night the same way he had appeared.

Eva was looking into the broken fragment of a mirror. She was combing her hair, and she'd cleaned off the dirt Lotte had rubbed on her face. How quickly all these events had left lines on her brow and around her lips; she'd grown old. She needed to sleep. She should throw some firewood into the stove, cuddle up to the children and get some sleep. But Eva knew she wouldn't be able to fall asleep. She had to stand guard over the sleeping. She was thinking about her eldest son, Heinz, walking through the night, thinking about herself, his mother, about his brother and sisters. Her mother's heart could feel that he was still alive. He had to be alive. And not because he was bringing food from Lithuania, absolutely not for that reason.

Eva sensed that it was getting light. The snowstorm had died down, and its whistling could no longer be heard. The first light of day was coming through the small window. All around there was silence, as if they were underwater. As if Eva had long ago gone under, and was combing her hair like a mermaid sitting in a giant shell. Eva touched her red curls again with her trembling, waxy, almost translucent fingers, the curls that Rudolph had so loved to kiss. *Where is he now, where is he now, where is he now?* She felt her heart being squeezed so hard that the pain became too much to bear, and it seemed that she'd go mad, go out of her mind, she'd start to shout and sob. She so wanted to weep, but where were her tears, where were they? Eva closed her eyes and lowered her head. She had to concentrate. She had to protect their children now, Rudolph's and hers. Before, she could have put her arms around his shoulders and not been afraid of anything. It wasn't so long ago that she'd been his girl, but now she had to be a mother – there was no room for self-pity. She put the letters and photographs back into the box and hid it under the bed again.

Eva didn't realise that she'd begun to pray, for Rudolph, for Heinz, for her children, for herself. Suddenly she heard something in the morning silence. Someone was approaching, coming closer with a heavy step, almost dragging their feet; the sound of snow crunching underfoot could be heard. Large snowflakes were falling. It was her son. It was as if Eva's blood had frozen. She was listening and waiting, listening and waiting.

The steps were coming closer.

Someone stopped at the door to the woodshed.

Helmut moaned in his sleep.

Someone knocked at the door, very gently. Eva rose from the bed, staggering from hunger and tiredness, and unbolted the door.

Heinz came in; her eldest child but still her little son, came in.

'Heinz, my dear child, it's you, oh Lord, how good, how good that you've come home, how we've been waiting for you, how afraid we've been for you, how we've missed you!' 'Don't cry, Mama, don't cry, yes, it's me, it's me, Mama, your Heinz. How have you been getting on without me?' 'You're frozen, my dear child, I'll boil some water, some hot water, there's nothing else, but at least there'll be some hot water.' 'Don't worry, Mama, you're hardly able to stand, Mama, sit down, I'll do it myself, I'll do it myself.' Heinz helped her to sit down on the bed. 'I've brought you something to eat from Lithuania…look how much there is of everything!' Eva could feel the pride in her boy's voice and tears choked her, the tears that had built up over all these days suddenly flooding out. Heinz was overwhelmed with emotion. 'Mama, don't cry, we're not going to die, look, here's some bread, some fatback, some onions!'

The boy took everything out of the canvas sack and spread it out on the wooden box that was being used as a table, the fatback carefully wrapped in scraps of cloth and paper, bread, onions, a piece of cheese, frozen potatoes, a paper bag of flour and some sugar cubes.

Eva swallowed her tears and bit into the handkerchief clasped in her fist. All she could do was look at her son, at her Heinz, still just a child.

'Mama, why are you so dirty?' asked her son.

'It's how it had to be, my child, it's how it had to be.'

Helmut, still asleep, began to sniff the air; he could smell the food. He awoke and sat up, rubbed his eyes with his small fists, then looked at the table with his large eyes full of surprise, wondering if he wasn't dreaming.

Then the girls woke up. They jumped off the bed and embraced Heinz, who was now proudly sitting by the stove, as if he were the real head of the family.

Then Auntie Lotte woke up.

The noise in the shed grew; everyone was rejoicing, full of wonder at the success of Heinz's journey, everyone was praising him. Auntie Lotte, who'd covered up her swollen eye with a scarf, was busy as a bee; she'd brought in some snow and was melting it on the stove that was blazing away. No one was going to save those few off-cuts of wood. The children had already had a taste of some of the bread and cheese, and were now waiting for pancakes made with real flour.

Heinz was telling his story, but Eva sensed that he was leaving out the terrible things that had happened to him, the horrible, unpleasant, demeaning things that he'd experienced, how afraid he'd been at night, in the middle of winter, in the middle of forests, in a foreign country, cold and hungry. No, her child wasn't relating any of that. No, he didn't want to scare or upset them. Besides, he understood that things here hadn't been easy either, perhaps even worse; after all, his mother's face hadn't been covered in soot for no reason, and Lotte hadn't been beaten for no reason. He began to understand everything.

'At first, I asked for things in Russian, like their soldiers: *khleb*, which means bread, and *salo*, which means fatback. But they didn't really want to give me anything. They looked at me like they didn't trust me, unfriendly, angry, so I then began asking them in German. They stopped chasing me off. I don't know, perhaps these people were different, perhaps because I was asking them in German…it seems to me that they respect us Germans more. Of course, I had to work. They have a hard life there, their cottages are small, dark, most of them without a wooden floor. Imagine – their chickens walk around inside! But they're good people, and there's food – bread, milk, fatback, no one's dying of hunger. And you're going to have everything you need, I'm going to go again and bring home more food.'

They could hear the barely disguised pride in Heinz's voice. Eva smiled. If only Rudolph knew what good children they were, how good they were.

'And I'll go with you! I'll go with you!' said the girls.

'And me,' said Helmut, wanting to be with his sisters.

Their mother smiled a sad smile, stroked Helmut's head and said, 'And if you go, who's going to be here with me?'

Helmut looked earnestly at his mother, and decided: 'Yes, I'll stay behind this time, but next time I'll go and Heinz will look after you.'

They were all laughing, but they stopped talking when Lotte's pancakes were ready. The children ate their fill, Helmut even used his finger to stuff a piece into his mouth.

'Don't hurry, children, don't hurry. After going hungry for so long, you'll get stomach ache,' said Lotte.

'No,' replied Helmut, his mouth full, 'the only thing my stomach aches from is hunger.' He laughed.

Heinz went to sit on the bed, saw his mother still smiling a little, the children still rejoicing in the good things he'd brought back. He caught his mother looking at him and smiled, and then, as if ashamed, he became serious, his head drooped and he began to snooze. Eva signalled to them not to make any noise, and covered Heinz with a blanket.

Heinz opened his eyes: 'Mama, sing to us.'

'Really, there's no need for that, my dear son. What songs am I supposed to sing?'

'Sing to us, sing to us, Mama!' Renate joined in.

Then Eva began to sing a beautiful and sad song, a song that a mother from any nation could have sung.

Renate stood up in the middle of the woodshed, raised

her arms and began to dance to her mother's singing, a slow swan-dance she'd made up herself.

Heinz's eyes started to close, and he fell asleep.

The morning was quiet and clear, there was no sign of yesterday's snowstorm.

In the morning silence, a mother's song flowed and hovered softly in the air.

THE FINAL MONTHS of the war and the ensuing events had been so hard to bear that people found it difficult to imagine that everything memory was able to retrieve from the past had really happened. It seemed that there had never been peace, cosy and tranquil homes, plenty of good food to eat, a warm place to live. Everything had fallen apart so quickly, especially relationships. No one could have imagined that they would walk so calmly past the bodies of the dead, not that it made any difference to the dead – they were no longer cold, no longer in pain. No one could ever have imagined that people could be possessed by such indifference, or this strange, almost slave-like despair mixed with helplessness, this resignation to their fate, the wish to fall asleep, to die. Eva saw with her own eyes how, when the soldiers of the Red Army moved in and the rapes, robberies and killings began, people walked straight into the Nemunas without so much as a backwards glance, straight into the cold and turbulent river. Drowning themselves. Whole families. What anguish, what pain must have gripped those people walking to their deaths. Mothers took their children with them. The water engulfed them, the river carried their bodies towards the sea. The waters of the river of despair washed also over the hearts of those left behind – everyone was desperate to find ways to help their family, their children, to survive, so that there was no room to think or worry about their neighbours and acquaintances. Everyone thought only of themselves and their own family.

Eva was lying on the plank-bed snuggled up to Brigitte, and remembering her own wedding. How she had met

Martha, the neighbourhood dancer and singer, with that sonorous voice. Everyone called Eva a 'Berliner' and considered her an oddity, with her soft hands unused to farm work. The neighbours found it strange that Rudolph had borrowed money to buy his young wife a piano of all things. But in spite of this, Martha and she got along. Eva had had to learn a lot of things in this small town. She wanted to be a good wife, a real housewife, but didn't always know how to behave in certain situations. Rudolph's father would suck on his pipe and look at his daughter-in-law through his half-closed eyes somewhat ironically, but indulgently. This reassured Eva, but knowing that people were always talking about her and making fun of her behind her back was not pleasant. Rudolph loved her, he would do anything for her and forgive her anything, but Eva knew that he was upset about the jokes they made about her being lazy and spoilt. Eva would sometimes cry at night; Rudolph would calm her down, and then they would make love, each loving the other all the more. Rudolph always took her side. He defended her and taught her how to go about things, without being insistent, without forcing her. But her husband alone wasn't enough; you couldn't live as if you were on a desert island with your man Friday. And that's how Martha had come into her life: it was she who introduced Eva to the women's club in town and to her other friends, who taught her how to do the woman's work on the farm, how to get on with certain neighbours and with people in the town. And it was only thanks to Martha that Eva started to fit in, like a young plant taking root in the life of the community. Martha became like a sister to her.

And then the war came, taking away their husbands, the men they loved. Eva and Martha, like all German women, had to work for the front, to help the war, for victory, the Reich and Hitler. Martha used to laugh all the time; she always used to say: 'Everything will soon be over, we will endure, we will live through this.' Whenever anxiety and despair took hold of Eva, whenever she became frightened for her children and Rudolph, Martha and her laughter were her only port of calm, her shelter. Eva was tortured by the thought that Martha had helped her so much, and now she was lying there while Martha perhaps didn't have the smallest crumb of bread, only yesterday's potato peels. If she'd managed to bring any back. If she hadn't dropped them while trying to escape from the drunken rapists. If she had even managed to get home at all. *And I'm lying here thinking only of myself and my children. Martha's helped us even when things were hard for her.* Even when the Russian army arrived, when Martha and her children were thrown out of their home, when their animals were taken from them, not even leaving them a single cow so that the children could have milk, when they took everything away and threw them out – even then, Martha had somehow managed to live with her children in one of the farm buildings for a while, to keep a couple of goats (not just one, but two!). And she had shared the milk with Eva's children.

Eva got up.

She had to go.

She had to go to Martha's.

'I'm going,' said Eva. 'I'm going. I can't let indifference win, I can't give in to apathy.'

'Where are you going?' asked Lotte. 'Where are you going? You need to rest, Eva.'

'I have to go to Martha's, I have to take Martha's children some food.'

'Your own children don't have anything to eat, Eva.'

'She was being chased by the soldiers, she helped me. I have to go to Martha's.'

'I'll go with you, Mama,' said Renate.

'Don't wake Heinz up.'

'I'll go too, are you listening, Mama? I'll help you,' said Monika.

'Stay behind, girls, look after your brothers. Make some hot tea. Lotte and I will go.'

'And I will go with you,' said Brigitte.

'Let's all put some soot on our faces,' said Lotte.

The wind that had quietened down in the early morning began to blow with renewed force, carrying a dusting of snow along the ground, across the frozen mud, in little whirling gusts. In the grey, restless sky three birds with black plumage were beating their wings, flying only they knew where and for what purpose.

Stooping against the wind, three dark figures were moving as quickly as they could. The road was straight and paved with rough-hewn stones. They still had several hundred metres to go on this road, then they had to turn left and pass the former wool-carding workshop, and then it wasn't far.

Apart from the birds in the sky, the women on the road and the wind, it was as if there were no other living beings in the world. After yesterday's shots and cries and the sound of the accordion, after the strange, incomprehensible din that had cut through the helplessness of winter, it was as if everyone was resting, exhausted. The women were walking along calmly. It was good that the wind was biting and icy, because it had driven anyone you didn't want to meet indoors.

An engine could be heard droning in the distance. The women instinctively bent down further, making themselves small, so that they'd look like feeble old women, shuffling with difficulty along the winter highway.

The droning came closer. It was a lorry, struggling along like a huge insect, which thank God didn't stop. It trundled on. The women saw that the lorry was full of people, numb with cold and only half alive, being taken somewhere to work. Lots of people were now being used to fill in the trenches, to cover up the remaining signs of war, the traumas of conflict. Those people were probably being driven somewhere outside the town.

The women reached the crossroads and turned left. It wasn't far now: there was the old wool-carding workshop, a bit further along the prayer house and the market square next to it, and beyond a cluster of tall poplars was Martha's home. Or what was now Martha's home – an add-on to the farm building.

As Eva, Brigitte and Lotte drew near they saw smoke coming from the chimney. It reassured them – it meant that things couldn't be that bad.

Lotte knocked, and rattled the door.

'It's us,' said Eva, 'it's us.'

The door opened. Grete, Martha's twelve-year-old daughter and a friend of Brigitte's, looked at the visitors with tears in her eyes. Her face was swollen; the signs of a beating could be clearly seen.

The women realised that there had been visitors during the night. They hurried across the threshold so as not to let in any more of the cold air.

Martha lay just inside on a wooden bed beside an improvised fireplace in which a fire was burning, covered with as many layers as could be found in their living quarters. Her boys – Albert, slightly younger than Heinz, and little Otto – cowered next to her in silence.

Brigitte put her arms around Grete. Eva said, 'We've brought you some things. Heinz came back from Lithuania, we've brought some potatoes, fatback and bread.'

Martha was lying motionless, and for a moment Eva thought that she was dead. But Grete took the gifts, hurried over to her mother and said, 'Auntie Eva has come, she's brought us something to eat, Mama.'

Martha raised her arm a little, but she wasn't strong enough to keep it up and let it fall. A small, barely discernible sound could be heard coming from her lips.

She said: 'The children…take care of the children…'

Grete was crying, dividing the food among the other children and putting a portion aside for her mother. The boys were stuffing their mouths with one thing after another, the fatback, the bread and even the raw potatoes.

'Leave some, leave some for tomorrow,' whispered Grete.

The visitors approached.

'Oh God, Martha,' the words poured out of Eva's mouth.

Martha turned her head a little. She had been so beautiful and proud, with a head crowned with light curly hair, radiant, and now she had been made to look ugly. She had been very badly beaten, she was barely recognisable, she was all swollen.

'Mama, eat some bread,' Grete said softly through her tears.

'Did the soldiers catch you?' asked Eva.

'No…they didn't catch me…but they came…later…several of them…thank God they didn't touch…the children…they only hit Grete…because…she was defending…me…'

'They went on and on all night, right until morning,' said Grete. 'I covered my brothers with the sheepskin, told them not to look and pressed their heads to the floor, and we cried, we heard everything... Mama, have a bit of bread...'

'I can't...' Martha murmured, and somehow managed to say, 'They knocked out my teeth...'

'I'll soften up the bread with some water, Mama, I'll make a gruel, Mama, just have a bit...'

'Eat, Martha. Heinz has come back from Lithuania, he says there's an abundance of everything there, and the people are kind. He'll be going back soon, maybe you'll let one of your children go with him?'

'I'll go to Lithuania with Heinz, I will, tell him,' said Albert. 'Let Grete stay with Mama, she needs help. And so does my brother.'

'You see, Martha, everything will be fine, the boys will go to Lithuania, they'll bring back food, we'll survive, you'll get better. You need to eat, Martha, otherwise there'll be nothing left of you.'

'Thank you, Eva...let the children eat, I don't want anything any more... I've had my fill... I asked them to shoot me...'

'Aren't you afraid of God, Martha? Think of the children!'

'I don't have...long to live... I can't... I don't want to live...'

'What are you saying, my dearest? You have to live, you have to,' said Auntie Lotte.

'We're going to joke and laugh yet. The time will come when the fields are in bloom, when these terrible days will end, and we'll laugh. Your laugh, Martha, your wonderful laugh, will ring out so loudly that it'll be heard on the other side of the river,' said Eva through her tears. Though she didn't believe it herself, as she gazed at Martha's swollen, torn mouth, black from clotted blood. Not even a mouth – just a gap between her lips, only a wound.

'No Eva, they killed my laugh.'

AN EARLY MORNING in winter. A goods train was standing on the railway embankment, with several wagons waiting in the sidings. Later, they were going to hook them up and turn the locomotive around, because further along, the rail-road tracks were different, narrower. That way lay Germany, East Prussia (the territory was now being called 'the lair of the fascist beast'). They would then hook on the locomotive – the last wagon now becoming the first – and the train would move across the Nemunas, to Lithuania on the other side of the river, and then on to the vast expanses of the USSR. The train chugged along with difficulty, loaded as it was with lathes, mechanical equipment, coal, antique furniture and all kinds of other things that formed the spoils of war. There were also the cattle wagons in which the war-weary soldiers would be returning home – *we'll be able to live, now that the horror of war has ended, this war that has taken millions of lives. We'll be able to live now.*

May God grant that happens, that they don't end up in labour camps, that on their return they'll find their relatives alive, that their houses haven't been burnt down, God grant that it be so.

Two small figures were coming down the hill, from the direction of the town. They dropped into the snow, and for a while they watched the goings-on by the train, the soldiers and railway men chatting, the women with their bundles asking to be taken to Lithuania, and perhaps even further. Then the boys (it's Heinz, and Martha's son Albert) got up from the snow. One of them was fumbling with a small, banged-up and burnt tank, and waved to the other to help. Albert rushed up and helped him to pull out a frozen piece

of tarpaulin. Then they waited. It seemed as if those soldiers smoking on the embankment would never go away, but
eventually they did. 'Now!' Heinz said, and they raced down
to the train as fast as they could, taking the tarpaulin with
them.

They ran up to one of the wagons, carefully looked around
and hid behind it. The man who looked after the trains was
checking something, tapping away with a special tool, walking along the side of the train.

The boys waited a bit until he'd walked off into the distance, and clambered up into the coal wagon.

Using bits of wood and flat pieces of iron which they'd
taken out of their rucksacks, they quietly began to dig into
the coal. It was hard work with the tools they had, because
the coal had frozen into large chunks; but the children were
determined, and once they'd managed to dig up an amount
that Heinz thought was enough, they laid the piece of tarpaulin down and folded it in half.

'Now you can lie down,' Heinz whispered into Albert's
ear. 'Get in.'

Albert lay down on the tarpaulin and covered himself
with the other half.

'Try to lie still for as long as you can,' his friend said, and
started pouring coal on top of him. He covered the whole of
the tarpaulin.

'Albert, lift up the tarpaulin. Lift it up.'

'I'm doing it, I'm doing it.' His voice sounded like it was
coming from the depths of the earth.

Albert raised one of the edges. Heinz helped him, then
climbed through the gap and lay down next to him under
the tarpaulin that was now covered with coal.

'It's really hard,' said Albert.

'The important thing is for us to start moving and to leave this place, then we can get out from under the tarpaulin. But it'll be very cold.'

The children snuggled up against one another, and their breath warmed the air a little. They could hear people laughing, calling out, then everything went quiet. Then came the sound of a large group of people passing by, before silence fell once more.

The last train moved off.

Its wheels began to move faster and faster.

'We're finally on our way to Lithuania,' said Albert. 'Do they really have everything there?'

'You'll see. Now, don't ask any more questions. Let's try to get some sleep, maybe we'll manage to nap for a bit.'

The train taking the boys to Lithuania chugged past wintry fields, swung around a small hill, crossed the river and disappeared into a tunnel.

RENATE WAS TIRED. She was sitting on a large wheel from an old lorry, breathing hard and watching the children play – Monika and Helmut, and that boy. They were throwing a ball around, playing a new game that the boy, their new friend, was teaching them using gestures and some incomprehensible language. He'd turned up several weeks ago. He came from far away, from Russia, and his family had settled into the pastor's old home. The house had once been enormous, but at the end of the war a bomb had destroyed part of it and killed the pastor. His family, like many other families, were seized by an uncontrollable fear and had moved out and escaped deep into Germany. They thought they could run away from the approaching Red Army. Who knew where those refugees were now? But Renate wasn't thinking about that, she was looking at her sister and brother and at the Russian boy. Their first meeting hadn't been very pleasant, because he had seemed aggressive; he'd attacked Helmut, pushed him over in the snow and pressed his face into the icy earth while shouting something. Renate rushed to help her brother, but starving children don't have much energy – luckily, Brigitte was close by. Brigitte showed that little Russian what's what. Helmut had a split lip, but he said that it had been a surprise attack, unexpected, otherwise he'd have shown that Russian who he was dealing with. Renate understood that Helmut felt like a failure. That's how boys reacted when they lost a fight. It wasn't even clear what the argument had been about, since the boy didn't know German and they knew no Russian. To begin with they hadn't got on, but then they gradually became friendlier,

44

and once, the boy's mother had even given them some bread. His mother was a very nice-looking woman with a sad face. *Meine Papa kaputt*, said the boy. When calling the boy, the woman would shout 'Boris, Boris!', and so the children also began calling him that.

Renate was sitting, looking at the other children, at the snow, at the darkening day. Evening was slowly drawing in, shadows lengthening. She knew that at home there was still some of the food left that Heinz had brought back. She would love a slice of bread with butter – she'd already forgotten the taste of butter, and though she tried hard to remember, the only things she could recall were the warmth of their house and Grandfather's cough, and how he'd carved whistles with his sharp knife. *Oh, if only there were some bread and butter now. A large slice. Or even a small one. Or just half a slice. Oh Lord, will there really never be any bread and butter again?*

The boys left the ball in the snow and climbed up into a lorry standing abandoned in the yard like an injured or dead animal – it had no wheels, and one of its doors had been pulled off. There was plenty of broken, abandoned machinery around now: lorries that didn't work, tanks that had been bombed, smashed to pieces, and bits of iron, the purpose of which the children had no way of knowing. The boys imagined they were driving along and being shot at; they hid in the back of the lorry, holding sticks that they pretended were guns. Boris climbed into the cabin, yanked and turned the steering wheel for a while, made the noise of an engine, jumped up and down – his vehicle went whistling through the fields of war, shooting at the fascists, manoeuvring through the deepest depressions in the earth and reaching the top of the tallest slopes.

Monika had slipped into a half-demolished building and disappeared for some time. Then, suddenly, her happy face reappeared, and she shouted: 'Renate, come here, see what I've found!' Renate went over and made her way across the beams lying on the floor. The house had no roof and there was snow inside, but there were also planks of wood, and they needed wood for the stove. Renate thought: *Let's get some firewood and go home quickly, Auntie Lotte will already have made something from what Heinz brought back. And perhaps Mama's got something from the soldiers' canteen.* The children had been told not to come back any earlier, because when they were at home and knew there were potatoes and bread and fatback, they'd want them – and the children's demands made Lotte lose her patience. 'Go and get some firewood,' she'd said. 'And don't hurry back, I'll make something to eat, but only in the evening.' Renate was wondering: *Is it evening yet?* The sky was turning a darker blue, and that had to mean it was evening now.

'Look,' said Monika, lifting up some sort of wooden lid. There were various metal things and weapons heaped up under it. Monika picked up a pistol, did something to it and all of a sudden there was a deafening sound and the gun fell out of the girl's hand. She was frightened, she couldn't breathe, her hands were shaking. 'My hands felt it,' she said to Renate. 'These are real weapons. Yes, real ones. The sound is still ringing in my ears!'

The boys appeared, drawn by the sound of the gunshot.

'Who fired the gun?'

'Monika.'

'Monika?'

'Look.'

Monika raised the planks. Boris whistled, and sharp,

46

mischievous sparks flashed in his eyes. He took an automatic and put it round his neck. It was so heavy that it was pulling him down. The boy aimed at the brick wall and pulled the trigger. Splinters of clay sprayed everywhere, and the sound was so loud that the children cowered, covering their ears.

Boris was laughing. He was happy. He liked weapons, he enjoyed shooting them. He showed the other children how the shots had made his hands shake and laughed again, he was so happy. He pulled the trigger again. When the noise died down, Renate shouted: 'Put the gun down! Don't shoot again!' Her ears hurt, but of course Boris didn't understand. And even if he had understood, he wasn't about to listen to some German girl.

Renate and Monika dashed outside. The ball was lying in the snow. Monika kicked it and said: 'I shouldn't have shown those weapons to anyone.'

The boys remained inside. No one was shooting any more. Renate called out: 'Helmut, Helmut! Let's go home, take some planks and let's go home.'

'In a minute!' replied Helmut. Then they came out carrying guns, and something else. That something else was a handful of grenades.

'Bomb, bomb,' said Boris.

'Helmut, put it back,' Monika told him sternly.

'Don't tell me what to do,' retorted Helmut.

'I'll tell Mama everything and then you're going to get it,' said Renate.

'Shut your mouth, you idiot,' said Helmut.

Boris threw everything into a pile, took the automatic, turned to Monika and began shouting, 'Hände hoch! Hände hoch!'

'Put the gun down,' said Monika firmly, but Boris didn't

understand. He turned to the lorry that had no wheels and pulled the trigger. The gun shook in his hands and the bullets whistled as they flew out, accompanied by a terrible noise. Boris aimed straight at the windows and carried on shooting until there were no more bullets left in the clip. He threw the weapon down, the sound of the bullets buzzing in everyone's ears. The girls were frightened, but Boris was happy, satisfied, as if possessed by a wild euphoria.

Helmut was trying to keep up with his friend; he was laughing too, although his heart was also probably full of fear. He didn't want Boris to shoot any more, but no way was he going to show that he was afraid like a girl. The lorry was watching the children with the empty eye sockets of what had once been the windscreen.

Boris had stopped shooting; he was piling things up. He was carrying planks. Helmut was helping him. They fetched an armful of old hay and the remnants of some kind of mattress, and threw them onto the pile. Boris pulled out a match and set it alight. The flame was very bright. Evening gradually descended over everything, and the girls warmed their hands by the fire. Boris was saying something, then he beckoned them and led them some distance away. He gestured to them to lie down in a sheltered place, and then went back, picked up a grenade, threw it into the fire, and quickly ran back to the girls. Helmut didn't really understand what was happening. Renate began shouting, 'Helmut, Helmut, come over here, quickly, run!' Monika too was shouting, 'Run, Helmut!'

But the boy, not sure what to do, didn't move. He didn't want to look like a coward or be made a fool of. He couldn't make out why his sisters and the Russian boy were telling him to hide, and so he just winked and stood there looking about him.

'Run, you idiot, come here now!' Monika screamed at him.

'I'm not an idiot!' her brother called back.

'Bomb, bomb!' shouted Boris. 'It's going to go off! It's going to go off!'

Although Helmut still didn't quite seem to believe them, he finally started walking in their direction. But he was walking slowly, dragging one foot after the other. The girls were furious with their idiot brother.

Finally, Helmut lay down behind a pile of stones.

They were twenty or thirty metres from the bonfire.

They waited.

Time passed.

There was no explosion.

Boris raised his head from time to time to look, but the fire was still burning and nothing was happening. The seconds passed slowly and they were getting cold, lying there in the snow.

'Perhaps it's not going to go off,' said Monika.

'Who told you it was a bomb?' asked Helmut. 'How does that Russian know it's a bomb? Perhaps it's just a piece of iron.'

Losing patience, Boris took a stone and threw it in the direction of the bonfire, but they were a long way away – it was hard to be accurate, and the stone fell about a metre short. Then Helmut threw a bit of brick, which landed a little closer.

Time passed and the evening slowly darkened. Boris got up from their shelter, picked up a long stick and cautiously moved closer. The fire was glowing, the bomb could clearly be seen in its jaws. But perhaps it wasn't a bomb, perhaps it was just a piece of iron. Boris carefully extended the long stick, trying to tap the damned thing, which simply wouldn't explode.

But he never reached the bomb.

The explosion was ear-shattering. It seemed to Renate that she'd fallen asleep for a moment and was now waking up. Smoke was whirling around. The buzzing in her head gradually died down. Helmut was saying something. Renate's hearing slowly came back – she could hear her brother moaning, 'What's going to happen now? What's going to happen now?' 'Shut your mouth, you idiot,' screamed Monika, 'shut your mouth!' Renate sat down, she felt even dizzier than usual.

The children approached the bonfire and saw that it was no longer there, and neither was Boris. It was as if someone had blown ash from the palm of a large hand. There was only the earth. A neat circle in the snow, a shallow hole, and nothing else. A little further away, there was something that looked like blood and a shirt, perhaps a shirt.

'Look,' said Monika.

In the trampled snow, mixed with soot and earth, lay a strange object. Like some horrible animal, its small legs spread wide.

Renate understood – it was Boris's hand.

They stared at the hand and felt an emptiness growing within them, gnawing at them from the inside, drowning out their voices and their breathing. It really was the boy's hand. It looked horribly pale, as if it were made of plastic.

Endless moments passed. Suddenly Renate realised what they had to do. She bent down, picked up the hand and, without saying anything, walked out of the abandoned yard. Monika and Helmut followed her. Renate didn't turn towards home. With small steps she hurried on, almost running, tripping and sliding in the snow; she went where the children didn't want to be, they didn't want to go there, but they followed their sister as if hypnotised.

Here was the pastor's house, one end of which had been destroyed by a bomb that had fallen from the sky. There was a light burning in the front room – the electricity had been turned back on again. Renate stopped when she reached the edge of the circle of light, and Monika and Helmut stopped behind her. They stood and looked at the snowflakes, which were flying around the lamp like small flies. The wind became stronger, making the lamp sway on the end of its thick wire. A gramophone was playing inside the house, someone was laughing, someone was telling a story, probably some jokes. They would be drinking vodka, or a looted bottle of wine.

Outside, the wind was getting stronger and stronger.

Renate stepped forward into the light and put Boris's dead hand on the front porch, right under the lamp. She waited a moment, then disappeared into the darkness.

Her sister and brother hurried after her.

They walked without speaking. They were each lost in their own thoughts, but all were thinking about what had just happened.

About Boris.

How would they explain to their mother that they had been firing guns and shooting an automatic weapon, and that instead of bringing home firewood for the stove, all they were bringing home was bad news?

Renate thought they were in a strange dream, perhaps in another world altogether, like the girl who went underground and met someone in a top hat and a hare playing chess. There was some way to go from the pastor's old house to their woodshed, and night had finally caught up with them. It was difficult to tell a wooden post or broken-down vehicle from a living person, but the children hurried on. They knew their town perfectly, even the way it was now, with the buildings that had collapsed, burnt down or been destroyed. After all, every day they darted around looking for firewood, and anything else that might be of use to them in their present miserable existence.

Finally, they reached home and stopped not far from the woodshed. They had to discuss what they were going to tell their mother, what their story was going to be. But what had happened was so terrible they knew they wouldn't be able to lie.

The children went inside and were astonished by what they saw. Their home was unexpectedly full. Their neighbour Martha was lying on her back on the bed, and looking at the low ceiling.

'I can't go on, I can't go on,' Martha whispered through her swollen lips. Her face was puffy, her eyes hardly visible.

'Good, you're finally home,' said Auntie Lotte in a low voice. 'We've got guests. We're going to live together. It'll be cramped, but at least it'll be warmer,' she tried to joke, the good-hearted Auntie Lotte. So serious and stern, and yet so full of sympathy for anyone who had suffered some misfortune. And nowadays everyone had suffered some misfortune.

'They were thrown out of their living quarters,' Brigitte explained to the children, 'just imagine – they hooked up a tractor and pulled it down. Perhaps not on purpose, perhaps they were drunk. It's lucky they didn't kill them.'

'The soldiers chased us out, they ordered us out,' said Grete. 'Mama said we should come here. She can hardly walk. Otto and I pulled her here on the sledge.'

Martha closed her eyes, stretched oddly and moaned.

'She's in pain, she's in pain the whole time,' said Grete through her tears. 'Mama, try to hold on, Mama, dearest mother, if I could I'd take on your pain...'

Otto was sitting next to his suffering mother like a little owl with drooping ears.

'I can't go on, I can't go on...' Martha moaned.

'How could they throw you out, how could they throw you out,' whispered Eva.

'They're capable of anything.'

Eva poured hot liquid into a cup. She'd boiled up some raspberry stalks, and the aroma of raspberry tea drifted through the air.

'We'll all fit in here somehow, we'll all fit in somehow, we just have to try, for the sake of the children. We have to survive,' she said, then put the cup of warm tea to Martha's lips. 'Drink, drink the tea, it'll warm you up a bit, you poor thing, and get some sleep, get some sleep...'

The boy looked at his mother and didn't say anything. It was as if he wasn't there.

Auntie Lotte made them something to eat from the food Heinz had brought back, and a gruel from dried potato peel – a gruel or a soup, call it what you want. Everyone held out their bowls and Lotte lovingly ladled the food into them for her own children and Eva's, as well as Martha's.

Renate looked at Otto gobbling the food down, and thought: *Heinz brought the food back for us, and now Grete and that little pig are going to eat everything.*

That night, Renate had a dream: she saw the old pastor's porch, and a bright electric light was shining down on the ground, the snowflakes were swirling and dancing, falling, and rising again. She heard the sound of laughter and music. Boris's perfect white hand was lying on the wooden floor, and then it turned into a flower of a kind she'd never seen before, with a sharp scent, unpleasant and cloying. The snow began to melt from the smell. But then an old, starving dog appeared, its bones sticking out. Somehow it had managed to avoid being caught. The dog snatched Boris's hand in its teeth and carried it off into the darkness.

The small, dead bodies of white insects swirled about in the air.

THE BOYS WALKED at a brisk pace, skirting the forest. All was quiet, apart from the powerful voice of a raven cawing from time to time. Heinz strode out in front as Albert tried his best not to fall behind. Yesterday, after their horrendous journey hiding in the coal wagon, they had finally found themselves in Lithuania. It wasn't at all what they had expected – it was the first time Heinz had got off the train in that particular place, and he had little idea what lay ahead of them. He was sorry to have left the tarpaulin behind in the wagon. They could have done with it now, but when the train stopped and they'd emerged from their cold hiding place, they were spotted by a railway worker who began to shout in some incomprehensible language and wave his arms about. The boys made off as quickly as they could, running even though their legs, numb from the cold, had other ideas – but they were being spurred on by fear, and the desire to survive at any cost. When they finally stopped to get their breath back, falling into the snow behind the bushes at the edge of a forest, they could no longer hear anything except their own breathing and the sound of their beating hearts. No one seemed to be chasing them.

'Are we in Lithuania?' asked Albert.

They were in Lithuania, of course, but neither of them knew where they should head now.

After a brief discussion, they decided to go in the opposite direction to the sun.

They walked for a good while. Eventually they reached a road, but there was no small town or even a village there, only a forest. Then the forest ended and the boys strode on, little black insects in the endless fields of white.

Eventually it began to get dark. The children were gripped by the fear of not finding a place to sleep. Surely they wouldn't have to lie down in the snow? But at last they came to a farmstead. The house and farm buildings were bathed in darkness, the snow in the yard had been shovelled and they could see that people lived there. As the boys drew closer they heard the barking of a guard dog, who greeted them fiercely, baring its fangs and trying to break free of its chain. The house seemed bleak and ominous, as if it were a den of thieves, but there was nothing else they could do. Heinz knocked on the door. There was no answering call and no one opened the door, so Heinz knocked again, this time more loudly.

They heard a man's angry voice; he must have been listening on the other side of the closed door, wondering who had found their way here and what they wanted. Heinz spoke in German, but inserted the few words of Lithuanian he had learnt, explaining they had got lost and were frozen and all they wanted was to get warm. The door finally opened, revealing a short, broad-shouldered man with dark hair, a grim expression on his face. His eyes were shining in the light of the paraffin lamp. The man raised the lamp, illuminating the boys' faces. He was silent for a while, then said: 'We have no room, there's no room here.'

Heinz began to plead; he was determined to change the mind of the devil himself, so long as he would allow them to stay the night. Then they heard the voice of a woman, who came to see what was happening. The man slammed the door in their faces, and the boys knew that they would find no shelter there. They would have to go on and sleep in the forest, perhaps try to make a fire and somehow survive the cold winter's night. Tomorrow they would move on, and hope that others in this country would be more hospitable. After a moment, however, the door unexpectedly opened again and the woman invited them to come in. The boys didn't need to be asked twice.

Inside it was stuffy, but warm. The woman talked a lot, explaining something in a low voice, as if not wanting to wake someone. The boys just nodded, not understanding anything very much but not wishing to disappoint her. There wasn't much room inside, and the travellers were offered benches to sleep on. There didn't seem to be any bedding for them, but they were given sheepskins and an old overcoat. The boys were freezing cold and tired. The warmth embraced them, and sleep came quickly. As he dozed off, Heinz could hear laughter, and some quiet, playful whispering, which then turned into a dream. He was sitting in a huge, empty meadow, waiting for his grandad. He appeared, but his legs were those of a horse. He was pawing at the earth, holding a pipe between his teeth. *Famine is coming, famine is coming.* His grandad – half-human, half-horse – seemed to be saying something, seemed to be neighing something, and Heinz wanted to ask a question but the centaur went away, disappearing into the distance. Heinz tried to catch up but his legs wouldn't carry him; they were as heavy as wood, and the boy understood that his grandad was leaving him – leaving him alone in the echoing, colourless void.

In the morning he woke up early, opened his eyes and saw the woman making a fire. He watched as the flames took hold and illuminated the dark kitchen, and he watched the shadows from the flames begin to dance on the pale walls. Heinz tried to get up, but the woman smiled and gently said something, making him understand that he could go back to sleep. The boy, trying not to fall off the narrow bench, carefully wrapped the sheepskin around him until he was like a caterpillar in a cocoon, and observed the woman's calm, everyday activities. It was pleasant and homely. Slowly his eyes began to close and, as the wood crackled softly in the stove, Heinz fell asleep again.

The boys were cheerfully marching along, their breath turning to white clouds in the cold air. The firs were clothed in snow, as if they were asleep and there was no death, and no war. The road was well travelled and not too slippery, and the going wasn't too hard, helped along as they were by a hearty meal and a good night's sleep. The woman had fed them well – when Heinz woke up for the second time, it was almost light and he saw that he'd been the only one still asleep. Embarrassed, he got up. Laughter trickled through the half-open door. Albert was using gestures to show the farmers' children something and they were falling about giggling. The house really wasn't large, and there were more than enough inhabitants: besides the master of the house, who was nowhere to be seen, there was his wife, and eight children. There might have been more, but Heinz only managed to count five girls and three boys. They were all foundlings, it seemed. The girls were laughing and telling Albert a story; one of them was waving her arms up and down as if they were wings, and must have wanted to say something about chickens or geese. It wasn't clear whether Albert understood what she was saying or not, but he was laughing too.

Heinz saw he wasn't going to be able to wash inside the house, so he went out and washed his face with snow. The

In the Shadow of Wolves

dog, who had greeted the boys so angrily, was now looking at Heinz and moving his head from side to side, apparently astonished. The master of the house appeared, not looking as stern as he had the night before – he smiled, and indicated with gestures and some sort of foreign language that Heinz was brave for washing in the snow. The man, pretending he was cold, shook his head, and waved his finger as if to say that it wasn't worth doing that. Or perhaps Heinz misunderstood; perhaps the only thing the man wanted to say was 'Don't catch a cold.'

When Heinz came back inside, the woman invited him to sit at the table. She'd boiled a whole mound of potatoes and everyone was eagerly waiting for breakfast. She put the steaming bowls of potatoes and dipping sauce on the tables in the kitchen and the main room. Heinz ate, taking his cue from the dark-haired man who had opened the door to them yesterday – the woman had fried some smoked fatback, and they dunked the potatoes in it. It was delicious. The only irritation was the girls, the daughters, who were snickering about how hungrily the German boys were attacking the food. There were plenty of potatoes, but the boys were ravenous. Albert ate with his head down, as if ashamed, and his bright-red ears were moving about in a peculiar way. The girls laughed, covering their mouths with their hands and whispering something to one another – undeterred by their mother's comments and their father's reproachful glances.

Yes, it was a pleasant day for striding out into the forest. Especially after a hearty meal and a good night's sleep.

Unfortunately, the farmers had been unable to offer them any work and it was clear that they couldn't stay on any longer. After all, the potatoes were probably everything that the large family had to eat. Well, and the fatback. The woman had given the boys a few potatoes for their journey – the first food they had received in Lithuania. Not a bad start at all.

The road twisted and descended into a valley. The children stopped for a while, adjusted their rucksacks and marched on. When asked about a village or small town, the master of the house had only pointed at the road and said something, waving his hand several times – it was clear what he was saying: 'Go straight on, and keep going straight on.' The boys did just that, but the forest was getting denser; there seemed to be no end to it. Heinz began to get worried. How much further would they have to go? Surely the forest had to end at some point. But who knew? After all, this wasn't Germany, this was Lithuania, a different country. Perhaps the forests here really were in fact endless.

An engine sounded somewhere behind them in the distance. The noise grew louder – someone was coming, perhaps a lorry carrying logs, or even soldiers.

'Hide!' Heinz shouted, and dived into the forest, with Albert following close behind. They fell into the snow and watched the road through the firs. A lorry appeared, then a second one and then a third. It was hard to say for sure, but they did seem to be military vehicles.

'Perhaps they could have taken us with them,' said Albert.

'Soldiers? No, I don't think so. It's probably best not to get in their way. They'll ask us where we're going and why we're in the middle of a forest, and we're not going to be able to tell them the truth. Besides, we speak German, so it's best they don't see us.'

The howling of the engines faded and the boys resumed their trek.

They'd been walking through the forest for some time. Albert was already tired, but he was managing and didn't complain.

'Do you feel something?' Heinz suddenly asked.

They stopped. Albert said nothing but merely looked at Heinz, who seemed to be listening intently.

'It feels like someone's watching us from the forest.'

'Perhaps it's a wolf,' said Albert.

Something moved among the trees, looming like the shadow of a big dog; now Heinz could see it too – no, it couldn't be a dog. It was important not to be scared, not to be frightened. They quickened their steps; there had to be a way out of this forest.

'How can there be wolves here?' asked Heinz. 'Don't be afraid of things you don't have to be afraid of.'

At last a wide stretch of land opened out in front of them, and they reached a fork in the road where a house appeared through some alders to their left. At last.

'Look, let's go there. There won't be any wolves there, only people,' said Heinz.

But they were soon disappointed. As they drew closer, the farmstead, which had looked so cosy from a distance, revealed itself to be bleak and abandoned.

One of the walls had fallen down, the sky was visible through the roof, and raspberry bushes grew in what had once been a room.

The boys looked about, a little frightened by this scene that was so far from welcoming.

In the middle of the old room, the snow had been trampled and a fire was burning, with a pot hanging over it. The leg of a calf or a deer was boiling in the pot, its hoof still attached.

'Look at this,' Albert said, pointing at the pot and the boiling hoof. Albert's voice was trembling, and his fear infected Heinz too. They were standing by the fire and looking around, but couldn't see anyone.

Plucking up his courage, Heinz asked, 'Hello, is anyone here?', but not too loudly, not quite sure of himself.

'Don't shout! Why are you shouting?' Albert rebuked his friend.

'Well, the fire didn't light itself.'

'And what if it's a forest creature, some kind of forest devil…?'

Suddenly someone behind them screamed, and their stomachs dropped. They leapt back and turned around. The scream was inhuman, they couldn't make out the words; it was so high-pitched and shrill that snow fell off the branches of the fir trees. The blade of a knife flashed right in front of Albert's face. He managed to avoid the blow, instinctively grabbing the child by its arm – and it *was* a boy's arm. Albert was wrestling with a small, ragged being, trying to defend himself from the sharp blade. He gripped the hand with the knife in it. The attacker kicked at him, screaming, but Heinz rushed up, seized the boy by the scruff of his neck and threw him to the ground. The boy managed to bite Albert's wrist and Albert hit him in the face with his other hand, forced his fingers open and took away the weapon.

Heinz pinned the boy to the ground. Heinz didn't recognise him, but we know that this was little Hansel, whom the Russian soldiers had taken pot-shots at as he crossed the ice on the Nemunas.

Hansel's eyes were like those of a madman. He was finding it difficult to breathe, and was still desperately struggling to break free.

'It's like he's rabid,' said Albert.

Heinz let Hansel go – he jumped up and ran into some bushes, disappearing in the undergrowth.

'He bit my hand!'

'He's like a wild beast. If he *is* rabid, you're going to get rabies as well,' said Heinz, and laughed. 'You were afraid of a wolf – perhaps that was a wolf cub. Maybe he ate the whole calf, and all that's left are the hooves.'

'It's a good knife, though.'

'I'd like to know where he got it. With a knife like that we won't have to be scared.'

The boys returned to the road and continued on their journey. They kept turning around, looking for the wild boy who had attacked them.

Albert's wound was smarting.

IT WAS MORNING, snow was falling lightly and the whole world was strangely silent. Renate was standing looking up at the sky, in which one could barely make out the drifting clouds – their contours blurred together, as if a painter had covered everything with pastel shades, with grey his main colour. Standing like this, it was easy to lose your balance, to lose track of where the earth ended and the sky began. Especially for a hungry child, who was always dizzy. Renate swayed for a moment, and leant against the wall of the barn to keep her balance; small, bright dots like golden insects were swimming before her eyes. She kept remembering Boris, and avoided the end of the town where his mother lived. It was strange, but the girl's conscience kept bothering her, as if she were the one who had done something wrong, as if she were to blame, as if some terrible force had blown that Russian boy away from his hand, blown him away and left nothing except a grotesque, bloody object, an unrecognisable small animal. Renate could picture Boris's mother looking for her son, crying as she walked through the town, despair engulfing her like black water. But perhaps she wasn't looking for him at all. She hadn't come to them to ask where Boris had gone, where her only son had disappeared to – though of course it was true that the unfortunate mother didn't know where the children lived. And as for the hand, Renate wasn't sure that it really was Boris's, but she did know that her dream hadn't been a lie: a dog had carried it off. Whenever she felt dizzy, her everyday existence became dreamlike. It was difficult to tell what was a dream and what was not; when she awoke, she longed to wake up again, for someone to be playing the piano again at home, and for Grandfather to be smoking his curved pipe, even if it reeked of tobacco, a smell she'd hated back then. Let him come back and be sitting in the sun. Smiling.

Time was moving slowly, as if being carried on the wind, on the breeze that lazily pushed along the grey, wintry clouds. Renate thought about Heinz. Oh, if only he could be home already! He would bring back some more fatback, potatoes and flour. She particularly loved the flour, because Auntie Lotte could make pancakes from it, each one yellow like a small sun. But she knew there was no point in hoping, in thinking that he was going to come back just because she wanted it to be so. No, that really wasn't going to happen; he wouldn't be coming back today, or tomorrow. They were going to be hungry and cold for a long time; there was no use in deceiving herself, in feeding herself with dreams, because it would only make the disappointment greater. Oh, if only her brother could succeed, if only he could, if only he didn't get lost in a snowstorm, if only he could find a warm and welcoming place to stay, a comfortable place where he could forget everything – his mother, Renate and everyone, everyone! *But that place might be a witch's lair, where you'd be fattened up like Hansel in the fairy tale, and there would be no one to defend you, my dear brother Heinz.* Renate would have liked to be there now, wherever her brother was. She'd be able to see through the witch's evil plans, to warn him and protect him.

Renate was walking along slowly, trudging through the fresh snowdrifts from last night. She touched the trunk of a linden tree with her hand and looked up again. Oh, those buds – they had all been picked off the lower branches. They were so tasty and, like hares, children had eaten them long ago, pulling down all the branches they could reach. Renate walked around the tree trunk, jumped up and tried to reach a branch, to grab hold of it and clamber up into the tree. If only she could. She tried once, tried again. She became tired; the branch was too high up. She threw her gloves down and tried again, but it was useless. She picked up a long stick and hit the linden tree's branches above her head with it. She hit them again, and eventually managed to bring down a large branch.

The buds were delicious, they melted in her mouth. But they were so small. Renate finished them all off and then began to gnaw on the bark.

At least it was something.

But all of a sudden she felt a stabbing pain in her mouth, and there was the salty taste of blood. She moved her tongue around her gums, and one of her teeth moved – it had almost fallen out. She pushed it back and forth, tugging on it until it came out. How easily it fell out, this milk tooth. *What if it doesn't grow back*, thought Renate, *then I'm going to be like an old woman, like Mama's friend Martha*. But no, Martha wasn't at all old, and her teeth hadn't fallen out on their own. Renate smiled, remembering how Helmut had cried when they'd pulled out his milk teeth. Renate wasn't going to cry; she found it funny, to be standing there with the tooth in her hand, and looked at it as if it were a precious stone. No, it wasn't a precious stone, but she could put it under her pillow before going to sleep, and in the morning a mouse would have left her a coin. But the girl suspected, though she didn't know why, that it wasn't going to happen this time.

A cow bellowed sadly in the barn. It seemed strange to Renate that a cow had bellowed just as she was thinking about her milk tooth. No, it wasn't theirs. Their cows had been confiscated a long time ago. This cow belonged to the Russians who were now living in their old home. It had been brought here from somewhere else, probably also taken from some family. It had been quiet for such a long time today, which was odd, because often it just bellowed and bellowed. It hardly got any hay, since the hay had also been confiscated, and all that was left was straw. The cow was bellowing from hunger. People could also bellow, but they knew there was no master they could call out to who would bring them something to eat.

Renate poked her head around the corner of the barn and saw the Russian woman who lived in their house locking the barn door. The lock was huge, and the key just as enormous. She hung the key around her neck, then lifted a pot from the ground and walked across the yard, along the path that had barely been cleared of snow. Renate was wondering whether there really could be milk in the pot. *Oh, when was the last time I had some warm, sweet, fresh milk to drink? Perhaps that wasn't even me?*

'Here, kitty kitty,' the woman's voice rang out, 'kitty kitty.' She was calling her cat, which she didn't allow to go far, because nowadays cats were also meat.

Renate followed her across the yard. It had been a part of her for so long and was so familiar, yet now it seemed foreign, as if it had betrayed its real owners.

'Kitty kitty,' the woman called lovingly to her pet.

Renate moved closer and stood still. She stood there and watched, waiting for something. She wanted to ask that woman to pour her a cup of milk, but how? Perhaps she should meow?

Finally the cat appeared. Looking well cared for and with a fluffy coat of fur, it yawned lazily and strolled over to the woman who was pouring some milk into a small bowl. She put it under her pet's nose. The cat made a face, licked itself, looked about. It seemed it was never going to get around to lapping up the milk, but then finally deigned to have a taste.

The woman turned to go and noticed Renate, who was staring at the cat lapping the milk with hungry eyes.

'Don't stare,' said the woman after a long pause. 'Go on, go home.'

But Renate was still looking at her, at this foreign woman, who had a fox fur thrown over her shoulders, who was probably dressed in everything she had found here, but bare-headed, with curlers still in her hair. Renate's eyes were clear blue, just like mother-of-pearl buttons.

'This is our house,' said Renate quietly.

The woman looked at her and said nothing.

'This is our home, we lived here.'

The woman picked up the cat and its bowl, took the pot and went inside.

Renate stood there without moving for what seemed like an eternity. She stood in this yard, frozen like a statue, where her brothers and sisters, her parents, her grandparents and her friends had once walked. She was probably not even waiting for anything as she stood there, but she didn't know where to go, her heart was full of pain. She felt that she had lost someone close to her for ever. She felt the cold breath of emptiness; yes, she was overcome by emptiness, like a deep well. Her soul was empty and echoing, like a well.

Then the door opened once more. The Russian woman stood on the doorstep and said in German: 'We're not to blame.' She held out a piece of bread wrapped in a news-paper and a bottle – perhaps there had once been vodka in it, only now it was filled not with vodka, but with milk.

Caw, CAW. A large bird with black plumage dislodged some snow from the top of a tall fir tree.

'Look how big it is,' said Albert, 'it's almost the size of a chicken.'

Caw, caw. The sound carried through the silent forest and far beyond, right up to the edge of the trees, to the farmsteads, towards which the boys were happily marching.

'I wonder if it's edible?'

'All birds are edible, why wouldn't it be edible if it's got feathers?'

The children made a fire, threw four potatoes into it, not even waiting for them to be properly done before pulling them out, tossing them like jugglers between the palms of their hands to cool them, and then hungrily wolfed them down, not leaving a single morsel. They then covered the fire with snow, hiding every trace of their having been there. Why? Perhaps because that was what the pioneers in America did in the books they read?

The raven looked down at the two small human figures, shook its head, then cawed again. A well-fed bird in a post-war world, almost a human being itself – full of human flesh.

Had the boys been travelling for a long while, or a short while? It was hard to say. Every inch of the forest looked the same, and the hunger gnawed away at them – what did two half-frozen potatoes do for two travellers such as them? But everything has to end sooner or later, and the forest unexpectedly began to thin out; light could be seen through the trees. A large field, a white plain opened up before them.

The boys raced each other to the edge of the forest and

then stopped, as if blinded by the endlessness of winter. But there, in the distance, they could see a farmstead surrounded by large old trees, smoke rising from a chimney.

The boys' hearts fluttered with joy, and they set off in the direction of the house and the people who lived there.

The raven circled above their heads and made a mighty sound, as if to say goodbye, then disappeared behind the fir trees.

The farmstead was quite big, with a wide yard, a barn and an orchard.

The boys turned into the yard. An enormous dog was barking by the animal shed. Not far from the dog lay a large heap of alders that someone had started to chop up.

A woman walked across the yard. She was rather old, but tall and straight-backed, with a warm, checked scarf around her head, and felt boots and galoshes on her feet. She didn't smile; she looked strong and stern. She was carrying a bucket, probably to feed the animals, perhaps pigs.

The boys said hello, and the woman stopped. She looked at them with distrust.

'Work, bread.' Heinz pronounced the words he had learnt in Lithuanian. 'We could do some work for you, for bread.'

'I don't have any work for you,' said the woman.

'The wood, we could cut up the wood.'

The woman didn't say anything for a while, as if evaluating the two would-be workers. She gave a crooked smile; it wasn't even clear if it was a smile, perhaps it was just the light crossing her stern face. But then she made a gesture as if to say, *Follow me.* The boys looked at one another and then followed the woman.

BRIGITTE, GRETE AND Auntie Lotte were hunting for rats in the ruins. The girls were carefully checking the holes and looking under the floorboards. At first it wasn't clear what they were looking for with such concentration, what they were hunting for, why they were moving so carefully, afraid to make a noise.

Auntie Lotte found something and made a sign to Grete and Brigitte, who came over and surrounded whatever it was that she had seen.

A rat ran out of a pile of rubbish.

Brigitte threw a rag over it.

Lotte rushed up, whacked the little animal moving under the rag, and killed it.

Most of the rats had died out too, only a few half-dead ones were left.

Brigitte took the dead rat and put it next to the two other dead rodents.

Another rabbit to add to the catch.

WATER WAS BOILING on the stove.

Auntie Lotte was skinning a rat.

Helmut and Monika were standing by with a bowl.

'What sort of animals are these, Auntie Lotte?'

'Little rabbits.'

'Do they taste good?'

'Very!'

'And why do they taste so good, Auntie Lotte?'

'Because during the summer the only food they eat is paradise apples.'

'But where are their big ears? I saw some pictures of them in a book, they had ears.'

'Big, fierce rabbits have big ears, small rabbits have small ears.'

'Why's that?'

'So that a fox won't see them hiding in the grass.'

Helmut and Monika laughed.

EVA TOLD HER young children to pay attention, to remember, to know where they came from and who they were.

'Wherever you end up, even if I'm no longer with you – remember,' she said, and the children understood that it was very important to remember who you are and where you came from.

'Repeat it, my dear child, repeat it and remember it.'

'I'm Monika Schukat, born in Gumbinnen* on 9 March 1936, daughter of Eva and Rudolph.'

'Don't forget the names of your brothers and sisters.'

'I am the daughter of Eva and Rudolph, and have two brothers: Helmut, my younger brother, and Heinz, my older brother. I also have two sisters, Brigitte and Renate.'

'And what nationality are you?'

'I'm German.'

'Now the rest of you, say who you are, say it and remember it, whatever happens. Go on, Renate, my dear girl.'

'I am Renate Schukat, born in Gumbinnen on 1 April 1939, daughter of Eva and Rudolph...'

'Helmut Schukat, born...born...' He couldn't remember any more and bowed his head in shame.

---

* Their surname, derived from Šukaitis, suggests that the family is of Lithuanian origin. Gumbinnen (Lithuanian: Gumbinė; Russian: Gusev) is a town in what was once East Prussia and is now Kaliningrad, about forty miles from the Lithuanian and Polish borders. Kristijonas Donelaitis (1714–1780), the Prussian–Lithuanian Lutheran pastor and author of the epic poem *The Seasons*, was born nearby in what was then called Lithuania Minor, a territory which in the eighteenth century had a sizable and culturally important Lithuanian minority in the Kingdom of Prussia.

Eva patiently continued: '...born in Gumbinnen on 13 April 1940, son of Eva and Rudolph. I have a brother whose name is Heinz and three sisters, Brigitte, Renate and Monika.'

'And I'm German,' said Helmut proudly.

Tears appeared in his mother's eyes.

'Why are you crying, Mama?'

'Try not to boast about being German. Just remember that it's what you are.'

THE HEAP OF firewood that Albert was building by the animal shed was growing larger.

Heinz was chopping the wood. He was tired, but was doing a good job of splitting the alder and asp.

'How come chopping is so easy for you, but I find it so hard?'

'Because you need to start from the thinner end and aim right at the core. Try it now, and I'll pile up the wood.'

Albert took the huge axe from Heinz, put a piece of wood on the chopping block and tried to split it, but once again failed.

The dog started barking happily. Its mistress had brought it some kind of potato gruel.

'She's feeding the dog, but doesn't want to give us anything.'

'Shh! Quiet, she'll hear us.'

The farmer's wife came out again, this time bearing chunky slices of black bread and a big steaming bowl of thick soup.

The woman was walking along the path towards the woodpile.

Albert was struggling with a huge log. He raised the axe above his shoulder, along with the piece of wood in which it was buried. He only just managed to hold on to the whole thing as he brought it down hard on the frozen chopping block. The wood split in half, and Albert wiped the sweat off his brow.

The woman said, in Lithuanian: 'You're working well, you need some sustenance.'

The boys turned, perhaps still not quite believing that

they were going to get something to eat. The woman put the steaming bowl, two spoons and some bread on the block.

They thanked her – Albert in German, Heinz in Lithuanian – and started to eat.

A soft smile, barely perceptible, lit up the woman's face. She watched the boys eat for a while and then turned back towards the house.

THE BARN DOOR opened and Heinz, Albert and the woman went inside.

The boys were carrying huge amounts of old bedding. The woman showed the boys the hayloft, where they could sleep. The boys climbed up the ladder. She spoke to them in Lithuanian, adding the odd word in German.

'I hope you won't be cold, but if you lie very close to each other you can keep warm. Just don't smoke, and don't light any matches. You mustn't light a fire and you can't smoke, do you understand?'

The boys understood that they couldn't light a fire, but they had to stay warm somehow.

'If you hear anything, don't make any noise and don't look out to see what it is, do you understand?' the woman said.

She went out, closed the heavy door and locked it from the outside.

Silence embraced the farmstead where the boys were spending the night. The stars and the moon shone over the snow-covered fields, which seemed to be sleeping. Somewhere in the distance, a dog barked.

Silence.

Then footsteps in the snow.

And the shadows of five armed men hurrying towards the farm.

Heinz and Albert were lying on the hay, wrapped in the thick blankets.

'This bread tastes so good,' said Heinz.

'Yes…so good.'

'Shall we have another bite?'

'Let's hold out until tomorrow. We might not get any tomorrow, so we should save it. And after all, we have to take some home, too.'

'We will take some home, we will.'

'Do you often think about your father?' asked Albert.

'Not often. Sometimes. I remember him showing us card tricks – he was very good at them. He said he'd teach me too, but he never got around to it.'

'It's not so bad for you, at least your father's still alive.'

'I don't know if he is. Who can ever know that? We haven't had a letter from him for about six months now.'

'I often think about my father. I wonder if I'll recognise him when I die? There are going to be lots of dead people, heaven will be full of them, there'll be so many dead people. Of course, they're not going to look like corpses, but when they say that you'll die and find yourself in heaven and you're going to meet your father, brother, all the people you love there – I don't believe it. It's not as if I'm going to be the only one walking among those millions of people and crying out "Papa, Papa!" Lots of other children, and adults, are going to be doing that too.'

The boys were silent for a while.

'That woman locked the door and I didn't even manage to go for a wee.'

'So climb down and have a wee.'

'I'm scared… Help me to get down. Don't laugh. I'm afraid of the dark.'

'We'll both go down, I need to go too.'

The boys went down the ladder without making a sound. They crept over to the door, but it was locked.

They had a wee somewhere in the dark.

Suddenly Heinz heard someone's footsteps crunching in the snow. He whispered to Albert to be quiet. Albert didn't understand and was about to reply, but Heinz put his hand over his mouth and hissed into his ear: 'Shh! Someone's coming.'

Through a gap in the door, the boys saw a shadow running up to the house and knocking on the window.

The door opened, and the shadow disappeared inside.

After a moment, the door opened again and they heard the sound of an eagle owl.

In the moonlight, more armed men moved along the path in the direction of the farmstead. They went into the house, with one of them remaining outside.

The boys glanced at each other, frightened, then noiselessly scurried back up the ladder to the hayloft.

It was just before dawn. Night was slowly fading, but the sky was still dark and the cold bit the girls' cheeks and noses. Renate and Monika had risen early and had some hot tea with a dry crust of bread, and were already in their place at the market. They were standing among the lines of carts, Renate holding a broom. The broom was a comfortable one to use. It had a well-made handle, and they had bought it, not made it themselves out of birch twigs. The girls had found a free spot and stood holding the broom in front of them, but no one had made an offer for it yet. No one needed it. They waited, getting colder and colder, then started stamping their feet to warm up. Renate was blowing her warm breath into the palms of her hands.

All around them, farmers from Lithuania were trading their goods: potatoes and bread, eggs and cheese, sour cream and fatback. People were bartering with them, offering their wares in exchange – drinking glasses prettily decorated with silver, a mirror, a coffee grinder, silverware, prized family possessions and jewellery. They wanted only one thing: food. A chance to survive, to live another day. The farmers were exchanging potatoes for these prized remnants from the past, which, now that nothing else was left, had been retrieved from their hiding places. Potatoes and fatback were now more valuable than the silver fragments of a peaceful and happy life long gone. A former teacher was trying to get food in exchange for books, heavy, beautifully bound volumes with maps and engraved plates. But no one needed books now.

A quarrel had broken out nearby. A little boy had stolen

a piece of bread and was running away, desperately gasping for air, but they had caught up with him and were whipping him. He stuffed the bread into his mouth so that they couldn't take it away from him.

'If we want to sell the broom, we'll have to walk around and offer it to people rather than just standing here until we freeze,' said Monika.

She took the broom from Renate and wandered about, stopping by almost every farmer, saying, 'Buy this fine broom, brought all the way from Berlin.'

But no one needed that wonderful broom from Berlin; they all shook their heads without so much as a word.

Monika lost her patience and handed the broom over to Renate. 'Here, take it and sell it if you want. I've had enough, I'm leaving for Lithuania today.'

'Mama won't let you go,' replied Renate.

'I'm not going to ask her.'

'Mama will cry if you go.'

Monika turned and left, leaving her younger sister in the midst of a maelstrom of people and snow. As the snowflakes swirled about her, Renate realised that, wherever Monika was going, she would not return. She shouted after her: 'Monika, Monika!' but Monika didn't turn around.

Renate was cold and tired. She was standing there, thinking about Heinz and Albert, who were now in Lithuania, and about Monika. Things were probably good there in Lithuania, on the other side of the river, but Renate couldn't leave her mama or Helmut. Somebody had to look after them.

She began making her way home and noticed a merry, peculiar-looking man playing music on a comb. His face was weathered and creased. Renate had never seen a man so wrinkled and old before. He was sitting in a cart with his legs crossed awkwardly, playing his music. His old wife was selling baskets that no one needed, and a few loaves of bread. She was cutting the bread into slices and asking ten roubles or ten marks for each – either currency was fine, but barter was best. A very thin, tall girl, wearing a man's coat that was too big for her, approached and pulled out a clock from under the coat. The old man's eyes lit up – it was beautiful, decorated with silver and copper, a wind-up alarm clock. The girl wanted more for it than they were willing to give, and the old couple wouldn't even discuss it, offering her two slices of the black rye bread, which weren't even particularly thick. The girl refused and tried to leave, but the old man was winding the clock, putting it up to his ear and listening to its ticking. He would have liked to have had it, but his wife wouldn't let him pay more for it. The girl took back the clock and went away to offer it to someone else.

The old man saw Renate staring at them with her large, shining eyes. Renate thought he was acting very strangely, he seemed almost mad. But then he called her over.

'Hey,' said the man, 'why are you staring at me? Do you want to sell me that broom?'

'Yes.'

'I don't need a broom. I can make as many brooms as I want myself.'

'But this broom is better, it's from Berlin,' Renate said, refusing to give up without a fight.

'Even if it's from Berlin, does that mean it sweeps any better? It sweeps the same as any other broom,' laughed the old man. 'We don't need a broom. Here, take some bread, and then off you go, we don't need your broom.'

Renate could hardly believe it, but the strange man was holding out a piece of bread. Renate snatched the bread and then quickly ran off, afraid that he might change his mind. Behind her, she could hear the man chuckling merrily.

Monika had decided not to go back home again, and was in the market on her own.

She walked for a long time, looking about her. The market was drawing to a close. She saw a weeping woman who was pleading with a Lithuanian farmer to buy her child, because she had four more waiting at home. 'He works hard, he's a good boy' – she was asking for some potatoes in exchange for him.

'Take pity on us, sir! God will help you. My boy is strong, he can work, he's not afraid of work. It's hard to give your child away, but I have four more waiting for me, and later, if you don't need him any more, he can come home…'

The farmer – fat, with a moustache – surveyed the child from all sides, checked his teeth, lifted his arms up. He thought the boy was too thin, and wouldn't agree to take him. The farmer's wife was trying not to listen to him, perhaps to avoid getting too upset. She started piling everything that was left over from the market into their cart – they were going home.

'Come on now, woman, how's the boy going to find his way home later, how on earth is he going to find you?'

'He's a very good boy, but we're starving, we're dying, we don't have anything to live on. How am I going to feed my little ones? Take him, sir, take him, all I want is half a sack of potatoes for him, only half a sack of potatoes.'

'What use is he going to be to me? He won't make any sort of a worker, he's small and weak, he'll need to be fed.

But what can I do? I'm not God, I can't help everyone, I too have to survive. Away you go – go, woman. Here, take a potato and go.'

The woman went off with the child to talk to other farmers.

Monika had observed the whole scene, and now plucked up the courage to go over to the farmer.

'Sir, are you from Lithuania?'

The farmer smiled, amused by the little girl's question.

'Yes, I'm from Lithuania, and what about it?'

'Sir, I very much want to go to Lithuania. I can work better than that boy, I don't need much, all I'll want is something to eat and I'll take any work at all, just tell me what to do and I'll do it.'

The man laughed, and said in Lithuanian: 'Did you hear that, wife? That woman wanted to sell me her child, but we can have this one for free.'

'And where's her mother?'

The man asked Monika: 'Where's your mother?'

'My mama told me to go to Lithuania. I'll do everything you tell me to do...' She stopped, and then added in a whisper: 'Sir, take me with you...'

The woman gave Monika a boiled egg.

Monika took it, opening her eyes wide, as though she were frightened.

The woman said, in German: 'Eat, eat. Don't be afraid. Get into the cart.'

Monika's eyes searched for Renate, but her sister was nowhere to be seen. She got into the cart and greedily ate the egg with almost all the shell still on it, and laughed.

The cart moved forward with the farmer at the reins, urging the horse on with a crack of his whip.

Monika was sitting next to the woman, who threw a sheepskin over the girl's lap.

'Are there paradise apples in Lithuania, ma'am?'

The woman smiled and said, 'There are in summer.'

They travelled into the distance, out into the world with all its busyness, bartering and biting cold.

And disappeared.

Renate hurried home to tell her family what she had seen at the market, but her mother just waved her away. Brigitte said: 'Later, Renate. Auntie Martha has died.'

Then Renate saw their neighbour lying in the corner. The children were kneeling around her, looking at their lifeless mother. Lotte and Eva were praying.

'Where's Monika?' asked Renate's mother.

'She's gone to Lithuania,' replied Renate.

Eva stared at the girl for a long while, then bowed her head and said nothing.

The stunned children were looking at their dead mother's body.

Auntie Lotte was quietly reading the Bible, while Renate's mother prayed.

Time passed. The light changed as the sun followed its course, invisible on the other side of the endless winter snowstorms and clouds. It was cold in the woodshed, cold and quiet. It was afternoon.

Monika hadn't come back – she must really have gone off to Lithuania, Renate thought.

'There's no point in waiting, we have to bury Martha,' said Lotte.

'The earth's frozen, we won't be able to bury her, we won't be able to dig a hole,' replied Eva.

'We'll manage somehow… We can't just leave her here, can we?'

Auntie Lotte struggled to her feet, took out some old

sheets and a tarpaulin from under the plank and laid the tarpaulin out. The children watched, frightened. Only Grete rushed over to help.

The women lifted up their neighbour's body. Using the last of their strength, they laid her on the sheet and wrapped her in it.

The women and children struggled to carry Martha's body through the driving snow in the yard, so they laid her on some planks of wood and began to pull.

Martha's youngest son, Otto, kept asking: 'Where are we taking Mama? Why is she wrapped up? Why isn't she saying anything? Where are we taking Mama?'

'Shut your mouth!' Grete screamed, and began to wail, her tears running in rivers down her cheeks.

'Why isn't she saying anything, why is she silent, why is she cold, why is she like a block of ice?'

Because Mama is no longer with us, Otto, because this is only a cold, dead body, it's not Mama any longer, it's a strange, cold thing, a corpse. That's why, Otto, that's why... But you can't say that to a small child, and it wouldn't make things any easier anyway.

'Go back inside, Otto.'

'Brigitte, take the little ones home and wait for us there,' said Auntie Lotte.

A STRANGE PROCESSION moved through the swirling snow: four figures, two larger and two smaller, were dragging a long bundle behind them.

'We have to bury her here.'

'No, Lotte, no…let's bury her in the consecrated earth of the cemetery.'

The whole Earth had been defiled long ago, the cemetery too.

Several crosses could be seen through the swirling snow.

Martha's funeral procession came into view: Eva, Lotte, Grete and Renate.

Despite everything, they had managed to drag the corpse to the cemetery.

The soil was frozen, so they were unable to dig a proper grave. Instead, they carved out a shallow ditch in the snow and laid the body in it, then covered it again. They made a cross out of twigs and stuck it in the snow, and the women said prayers and crossed themselves.

'God forbid that we should ever suffer this kind of death, this kind of funeral…'

'Who knows, Eva. You can see what's happening around us. Who knows what awaits us. We're not going to be able to choose the time or place.'

Grete had fallen to her knees in the snow that had just been used to cover her mother. She was wailing.

Auntie Lotte lifted the girl up. 'Let's go, let's go, my dear little Grete.'

'She'll be cold here.'

'She's in a better place now than we are.'

———

Strange silhouettes were moving across the endless white fields,
the snow was dancing and playing, carried by the wind,
the cemetery could occasionally be seen through
the swirling snowflakes,
it was getting dark,
the figures of the women and children were
like ghosts swaying in the wind...

IT WAS A cold, clear winter's day. A horse-drawn sleigh was flying along at a lively pace, in its driver's seat an elderly man. On the wide bench behind him sat a woman, and next to her Heinz and Albert. The boys were now dressed in warmer clothes.

The man stopped the horse with a loud 'whoa!' when he reached a turning that led off the country road.

'There's a small town straight ahead, about two kilometres away,' the man said in Lithuanian. Then he added a few words in German, to make sure the boys understood. 'Two kilometres, town,' said the man.

The boys thanked them in Lithuanian and got out.

The woman sighed. 'You poor boys, where are you going to go?'

The boys thanked them again, happy because their bags were now quite a bit fuller than before.

The sleigh continued towards the forest and disappeared, bells tinkling.

Heinz and Albert waved to the couple who had given them a lift, and turned in the direction pointed out by the farmer.

The two young German boys walked across the empty fields that glistened in the sunlight.

They saw a farmstead surrounded by orchards. From a chimney, smoke was rising straight up into the sky.

They turned towards it.

As the boys approached the gate, a fierce black dog started barking furiously.

'I'm sure we'll earn a good bit here.'

'Be happy, Mama, we're going to bring back bread!'

They opened the gate.

The owner of the house came out, probably to see what his dog was getting so excited about. He was a stocky man. He looked at them angrily.

Warily, the boys edged forward.

'Good afternoon—'

'What do you want? We don't need any tramps here, get out!'

Albert, who didn't understand any Lithuanian, asked Heinz:'What's he saying?'

'I don't understand.'

'You don't understand what I'm saying? Get out, get out of here, get away, get away from here! Tramps.'

'We could work for you—'

'You Germans, go back to your Germany, I don't need any Germans. Get out or I'll set the dog on you.'

Albert quietly said:'He's very angry, Heinz. Let's go.'

'We'd better run, he's going to set the dog on us,' said Heinz, afraid.

Heinz lost no time and started running. Albert, a little confused, understood too late that the farmer had already released the enormous dog.

The children ran as fast as they could. The dog, black and terrifying, was running straight at them. Realising that he wasn't going to able to get out of the yard in time, Albert turned to it and took out the knife.

He raised his weapon. He wasn't going to give in, he was going to defeat that beast.

Heinz was running, calling to his friend, but Albert wasn't listening. Heinz kept running towards the forest.

The dog attacked. The boy and the beast were entwined, the dog yelped pitifully, there was blood on the snow – the boy had cut the dog's throat.

The boy threw the dog off him. They were both covered in blood, and the boy was still holding the weapon in his hand.

The farmer came running up with a rope in his hand and started to whip the boy with it, who threw himself at the farmer like a madman and slashed his hand with the knife. The farmer screamed and jumped back, bleeding.

The boy stood there, covered in dog bites and with a bloody knife in his hand, shouting: 'I'll kill you, I'll kill you, I'll kill you!'

The farmer decided that the boy must be rabid. He backed away, full of rage, then ran home to get his gun.

The boy staggered out through the gate.

Once outside, he looked for Heinz, but he was nowhere to be seen. Albert set off down the path, trying to get away from the farm as quickly as possible.

The farmer came flying out of the farmstead, aimed the gun and, with shaking hands, pulled the trigger – but Albert was too far away. The bullet missed him, but the boy threw himself down on the path just in case.

Heinz, already in the forest, heard the shot. He didn't know what direction to go in, but kept moving forward, to get as far away as he could.

Albert got up, looked back and saw the farmer standing there, gazing at his dog. From a distance it looked just like a faint black dot.

Alvydas Šlepikas

The boys were searching for one another, Heinz among the trees and Albert walking down a track. From time to time the boys called out, but they had already lost each other.

Exhausted, Heinz sat down on a tree trunk. He carefully unwrapped the bread from its newspaper and broke a chunk off one of the slices, took a small piece of the fatback and ate hungrily.

94

IT WAS GETTING dark. The forest was silent and frightening.

Albert was walking along a path. He was tired. He'd probably been walking all day. There were no people around, only forest. Suddenly, the boy's surroundings began to look familiar. He was tired, terribly tired – surely he would never reach the farmstead where the girls had made fun of him, where they'd had potatoes with fried bits of fatback for breakfast? But yes, these places really were familiar to him, he couldn't be mistaken.

The roof of a house appeared through the trees and the snow, and despair engulfed the boy's heart like cold water – no, it wasn't the friendly house, it was the uninhabited one, where that wild boy had attacked them. This is where Albert had taken the knife away from their attacker, the knife he had used to defend himself against the black dog. There was no door, no windows, not even a roof – this was no place to spend the night.

He approached the farmstead nervously, watchfully, so that little Hansel couldn't take him by surprise.

For a few moments all was quiet. Nobody jumped out at him. There was not a single sound.

Albert found the place where the fire had been, the pot with the now-frozen broth in it, and little Hansel, lying on his back, dead, frozen into a slab of ice.

One of his eye sockets was filled with soft snow. From the other one, an icy eye looked up at the sky in amazement.

RENATE WAS LOOKING up at the branches of the linden tree. Everything had already been eaten, she couldn't reach any higher. She was picking at the cold, frozen bark and chewing on it. Hunger was gnawing at her, like a rat in her chest. She was thinking how good it would be to go to the forest, where there were bound to be trees with lots of buds; she was thinking that if only spring arrived earlier it would be possible to find all kinds of herbs, sorrel and berries. The wind was penetrating the girl's clothes and burning her face. Because of her constant dizziness, she was walking carefully so as not to fall down on her way to her 'home', the woodshed. Life there was so hard to endure, with Helmut's endless moaning, Otto's perpetual whimpering and sobbing as Grete mutely held him close, and rocked him as if she wanted him to fall asleep forever. But at least there was hot water there, and tea from the raspberry stalks in the orchard, which had almost been stripped bare.

Renate entered the woodshed. It was dark inside, with only the one small window to let in the light. Auntie Lotte was holding up Eva's feverish head and helping her sip the raspberry tea. As Renate had expected, Helmut was crying and continuously repeating the same refrain like a stuck gramophone record: 'I want to eat, I want to eat, I want to eat, I want to eat.' For a while he stopped, then started up again: 'I want to eat.'

Eva couldn't bear it any longer, and all of a sudden began shouting as loudly as she could and as much as her weakened state allowed: 'Why are you always moaning? It's not as if no one else wants to eat, as if everyone else is full. I too want to eat, so what am I supposed to do? You're always eating, can't you just sleep?' Eva was shouting and choking on her angry, unmotherly words, choking on her tears of despair; Lotte was trying to calm her down, to hush her, and then Eva began shouting at her as well. She was twisting and turning on her bed, as if some unseen, horrific beast was trying to break out of her – perhaps Hunger itself, which she was carrying beneath her heart.

Renate's older sister Brigitte got up from where she was sitting and said: 'I'll bring back some food for you, I will!' Then she walked past Renate, and went outside. The door closed behind her, but the crunching sound of her footsteps in the snow could still be heard. Renate wanted to calm her mother and Helmut down – she too would have liked to cry, to be comforted – but how could she do that? It was horrible, every day was horrible, and getting more and more so. She ran after Brigitte.

Renate dashed out the door and looked around her – her older sister had already gone quite far, marching at a determined, steady pace.

'Where are you going, wait, wait for me, Brigitte!' shouted Renate and chased after her, stumbling as she went.

'Where are you going, what are you going to do?'

'If Heinz can bring back food from Lithuania, so can I. I can't stand Helmut's moaning and Mama's scolding any more, I can't, I can't bear it.'

Brigitte didn't slow down, and Renate tried not to fall behind.

'I feel the same, Brigitte, you're right, take me with you.'

Brigitte strode on without a word.

The road was not short and Renate was barely managing to keep up, but she was determined not to get left behind.

They crossed a deserted space, squeezed through a metal fence, and then the railway was not far away at all. They were walking along keeping their eyes on the ground, trying to avoid the soldiers at the station who seemed to be waiting for something, leaning on their guns, smoking stinking tobacco, joking around. Women with large bundles tied up in sheets were also waiting – perhaps for a train, perhaps for a person. The railway workers were tapping on the wheels of the trains with their hammers.

The girls slipped between the carriages of one of the trains, and continued over to another line of trains. As they walked along the tracks, they saw a second group of soldiers, who were evidently on their way home to Russia, by way of Lithuania. They were boarding a carriage with wooden sides, carrying their suitcases and bundles with them.

'I'm sure this train will get us to where we need to go,' said Brigitte.

They walked along the train, searching for an open wagon. Eventually Brigitte spotted one. The girls looked around and quickly climbed inside – Brigitte went first, and then Renate gripped her sister's hand and somehow managed to clamber in after her. It was dim inside the wagon, but their eyes soon adjusted. Hay and straw were piled up at the front end, and there were several piles of manure on the floor; it must have been used to transport horses.

'We need to hide in the straw,' said Brigitte.

Voices could be heard outside, speaking in Russian and laughing. The girls heard people approaching. They hid in the hay as best they could. Suddenly the doors of the wagon burst open, light flooded in and one after another soldiers started climbing into the wagon. They were glad, they were going home, they were returning victorious from the war.

Renate could see them joking and jostling each other, punching one another in the back; there were about ten of them, perhaps more. An officer shouted something to them from outside. They answered him in a serious voice and one of them saluted him. They didn't close the doors to the wagon completely, but left a gap. Some sat on the floor with their legs hanging out of the open doors and lit their roll-ups; others put their suitcases on the floor, took food out of their bags and suitcases and started eating. Others collapsed onto the straw, one of them almost touching Renate. The girl was trying not to breathe, she could smell tobacco coming from the soldier, but he hadn't noticed her. He was tired and trying to get some sleep.

At last the train moved off, but then the soldier turned onto his side and felt something alive right next to him in the straw. Surprised, he sat up and saw that it was a girl. Renate's eyes were wide open and full of fear. The soldier said something to her; the girl, horrified that she'd been seen, leapt up from the hay and ran towards the wagon doors. The soldiers were so surprised that they made no move to stop her, and she jumped from the train, which was already travelling at a high speed. Someone shouted something after her in Russian. The soldiers, startled by the incident but now alert, found Brigitte. Brigitte tried to avoid being caught by them; she wanted to escape, to jump out after her sister, but the soldiers wouldn't let her. They were saying, 'Don't be afraid, why are you afraid? We're not going to do anything to you, you'll kill yourself, don't jump, you'll kill yourself!'

'My sister, my sister,' shouted Brigitte, 'my sister Renate, let me go, let me go!'

The soldiers tried desperately to stop her.

'Calm down, calm down, you'll kill yourself – *kaputt, kaputt*! You can't jump, girl, we're not going to do anything to you, why are you afraid? Don't be afraid!'

Brigitte fell silent. The train was moving along quickly, going faster and faster, and through the open doors the older sister could see a bundle of clothes far behind and knew that it was her sister. It was Renate, lying on the snow and ice, lying there as if dead.

Renate could hear the train in the distance. She slowly got up. A trickle of blood ran down from her temple. After she'd jumped from the train she'd hit her head on a block of ice, but she was gradually recovering. The world stopped whirling, flying, swaying, the black spots disappeared, and then Renate understood: Brigitte was on her way to Lithuania on her own.

FAMINE AND COLD can defeat people, break them. They become empty metal mechanisms who don't hope for anything, aren't afraid of anything and aren't surprised by anything. Time passes slowly without any variation, and movements become mechanical, as do thoughts.

'It'd be better for him if he were dead,' said Auntie Lotte.

Helmut was moaning again, saying the same thing over and over. His moaning was like a drill.

'I want to die too,' said Eva.

'They're coming,' sighed Lotte, 'they're coming.'

Footsteps could be heard in the distance, voices. They really were coming – perhaps the hearing of a hungry person is so sharp that they are able to hear through walls.

Soldiers.

They knocked on the door. But the door hadn't been bolted for a long time and they let themselves in, a red-cheeked lieutenant with thick, bushy eyebrows, and a couple of other soldiers.

'Collect your things,' he said in Russian. 'Get your things together, and let's go.'

Where to? asked Lotte. *Where will we go to from our house, from our woodshed?* But no, she didn't ask, she just wanted to ask, but what would have been the point? There was none – he'd told them to get their things together, so that's what they had to do.

'My children are out, my girls aren't here,' said Eva. 'We have to wait for my children.'

'We're not going to wait for your children,' said the lieutenant. 'We're not going to wait, there's no time to wait.'

'Where are you taking us?' asked Lotte.

'We're gathering everyone at headquarters, and then you'll be taken to work.'

'Work?'

'You'll get food coupons and some bread in return. Someone's got to fill in the trenches and the dugouts left over from the war.'

Auntie Lotte and Grete gathered what they could: clothes, footwear, anything that might help in the severe cold. Lotte was sorry to say goodbye to the metal stove, but how could they take it with them?

'Hurry up, how long do you expect us to wait?' the lieutenant said impatiently.

Finally they went into the yard, where there was a commotion: the Russian woman's cow could hardly stand up and wasn't giving any more milk. A man was pulling it out of the barn into the yard.

'Shoot the animal,' he said. 'Shoot it.'

'It has to be fed. See what happens if you don't feed it? All that's left of it are bones and eyes,' laughed the elderly moustachioed soldier.

'Feed it on what? What can we feed it, when there's no fodder? Shoot it,' said the woman.

The soldier took aim and pulled the trigger. The shot echoed, loud and sharp. The animal collapsed and didn't get up again.

'At least we'll have some meat now,' said the cow's owner.

Otto was looking wide-eyed at the dead animal. Grete wanted to hurry her brother along, and pushed him.

'Sit in the sled, Otto, sit down.'

The soldiers drove the women and children on. An icy wind, snow. The ruins of houses around them, burnt-down animal sheds, broken wagons, boxes, suitcases ripped open, broken prams. The snow was dirty with soot, and black flecks of blood, or oil stains.

There were frozen corpses along the side of the road, and at a little distance from the road people were sitting on logs. The children asked: 'Why are they doing that, what are they waiting for?' Lotte explained: 'They're dead, they couldn't walk any more, they sat down and froze.'

Lotte and Grete were pulling the sled in which Helmut and Otto were sitting, Eva walking behind; her eyes were closing, her legs felt like tree trunks, cold and hunger were gnawing at her like an iron worm that had settled in her chest, and all she wanted was to die.

RENATE WAS WALKING home. On the way she came across a group of drunk soldiers who seemed to want to catch her, but they were too drunk. One of them had lain down on the road, another one was laughing, and they started fighting among themselves. She hurried on to get away from them.

She arrived back home, hungry and tired. Outside, a snowstorm was raging.

There was no one in the woodshed, no one at home. The girl called out.

'Mama, Auntie Lotte! Mama, Auntie Lotte!'

It was cold inside.

She went out into the yard, where she saw the fat neighbour carrying a huge piece of meat in her arms.

Renate walked around the small town looking for her family. She went to the marketplace, now empty, and down several more streets. In the end she turned back in the direction of home.

A fire was crackling in the metal stove. Renate sat beside it, trying to warm up.

She wrapped her rags tightly around her and fell asleep.

She was dreaming of peace. She saw her smiling mother, who was sitting in a summer meadow, teaching her to read from a beautiful book. Suddenly, a cloud appeared in the sky and her mother became scared. Renate wanted to see what had frightened her mother, but she wouldn't allow her to – she turned Renate's head away. They were overwhelmed with such sadness, such fear, that both the meadow and the book became twisted, as if drying up, withered like a piece of old skin, and then everything began to disintegrate and her mother's face melted as if made of wax.

HEINZ WAS TIRED. He hadn't had any food or sleep in a long while, and was barely able to walk. He arrived at a town where there was a market. A cheerful farmer caught his attention. He seemed kind-hearted. The boy went up to him and asked for a little bread. The man gave him some. He also offered him some strong, home-made alcohol, but the boy didn't take it. He asked the man if he needed a helper. The man told him to lift a basket with potatoes in it. Although he was tired, the boy began to lift. 'Lift it, lift it, lift it,' the farmer repeated, egging him on and clapping his hands with delight. When the boy had lifted the basket above his head, the man shouted, 'Bravo, bravo!' A woman, frightened by the shouts, turned around, crossed herself and hurried away. The man said: 'Wait a bit, I'll have sold the potatoes soon, and then we can go home. I need workers like you. I really need good, strong children like you. My wife will be happy, she'll be really happy – the two of us will go home together, and then you'll have to keep up. We have a lot of work at home, a lot, and you're a real man. You'll be my helper.'

Now they were working together – the boy selling the potatoes, doing as he was told. The farmer kept drinking the alcohol; he was quite drunk, and occasionally broke into song and told stories, but the child's knowledge of Lithuanian was still poor.

The last of the potatoes were sold, and they started off for the farmer's home in the horse-drawn cart. The farmer was singing. After a while he lay down and covered himself with a sheepskin. The boy was frightened – if they got lost, who would lead the horse back in the right direction? But the farmer said that it knew its way home.

Some passing soldiers gave the boy sitting in the cart a suspicious look. The farmer was asleep.

Heinz and the farmer were travelling along a dirt path that led far away into the distance. The thawing snow had turned to slush.

For a while they travelled through fields, but then suddenly, and without hesitation, the horse turned right, down a path into the forest.

It was so quiet among the trees that a thought unexpectedly popped into Heinz's head that it could only be this quiet under water – but just then two large jays flew screeching over the boy's head, like giant bullets chasing each other. They grazed the branches of a fir tree, and snow fell down like flour. The boy flinched, but the horse kept going at the same pace. The cart's owner emitted an occasional snore. The boy found it puzzling that the man didn't seem to be afraid of anything.

They travelled along for a good while, the horse turning once or twice down even narrower paths. Garlands of fir trees blocked out the sky, and it grew dark. The boy was scared, but comforted himself with the thought that if they were in any danger the man wouldn't be sleeping. The forest thinned out again, and they passed a few farmsteads, but the country still seemed deserted, as if everything around them was dead. Only the occasional, thin call of a crossbill could be heard, or the echo of a raven's powerful, soothing caw coming from somewhere in the distance.

The horse, as if obeying an unspoken command, stopped when it reached a small bridge over a stream that babbled along under the snow. The boy didn't know what he should do now – they couldn't exactly stop here forever in the middle of a hollow, surrounded by forest. But no sooner had he thought this than the owner suddenly woke up, and jumped down from the cart with a strange huffing and puffing, his breath coming out of his mouth in clouds. Then he urinated contentedly by the side of the path. Afterwards he stood for a moment, stretched and yawned. He did up his trousers and turned around, and as he was getting ready to climb back into the cart and carry on with his journey, he saw the boy. The man stood transfixed. Heinz looked at him, unable to work out what was happening.

'Where did you come from?' asked the man. 'What are you doing in my wagon?'

Heinz attempted to explain in German and a little in Lithuanian that they were travelling together, and that they had agreed that he would work on his farm.

'What farm? I don't need any workers, we do everything ourselves, that's nonsense. Why should we need to hire any boys?'

'But we agreed, you said that you needed me, you said I'd be of help, you said you liked me, that I'm a good worker.'

'No, no, no, no, we don't need any workers, we don't, and anyway, what sort of a worker would you be? No, no, get down from my cart, what's my wife going to say if I bring you home? She'll throw us both out!'

Heinz, still unable to believe what was happening, thinking that perhaps he hadn't understood the man properly, got down from the cart slowly, as if hoping to hear the man urge him to stay, tell him that they would go on together.

But no, no one was urging him to stay, no one was saying they should go on together. The boy looked at the man, but the drunkard, who had by now sobered up, waved his whip over his head, muttered something, and shook his head as if in disbelief that he could have gotten up to such nonsense while he was drunk: *As if I'm going to hire a German boy.* The whip whistled in the air and the cart moved on, pulled by the obedient bay horse.

And here was Heinz now, all alone in the middle of the wild forest, in the middle of a winter with no end in sight.

It was slowly getting dark. The snow on the branches of the trees and along the road was turning blue and further in, where the forest was denser, it was already completely black.

The boy was walking along the forest edge, disquiet and despair falling on his head like heavy snowflakes. The real snowflakes, soft and fluffy like balls of cotton wool, were the size of a child's palm. Heinz didn't want to go on, he just wanted to lie down in this snow of oblivion and remain there, covered in snow, for all eternity; but the boy knew that if he fell asleep he would never wake up again, and his mother and Renate, Helmut, Monika and Brigitte were waiting for him to come home, waiting for him as they starved to death, and so Heinz had to return, he had to go back.

He continued walking at the same pace. It was already dark and the forest scared him. Suddenly there was a flash, as if a small but bright light was shining far away.

Heinz gathered what strength he had left and headed towards the small light. It disappeared and reappeared, and the boy realised that the trees were hiding the mysterious beacon. At last he reached it. It wasn't a bonfire as he'd first thought – no, it was coming from a paraffin lamp in a window. The rest of the cottage was dark and bleak.

The boy cautiously approached, worried that there might be a guard dog. But there didn't seem to be one. He crept up to the window and tried to look inside, but was unable to see anything through the ice that covered the pane.

He listened. He thought he could hear laughter.

He went to the door and knocked.

No one came to open the door, and Heinz knocked again, louder this time.

He heard steps approaching, and a man's angry voice. 'Who is it?'

'I'm lost, please help me,' the boy answered.

Long torturous moments passed, and just when he'd given up any hope that the door would open, he heard the sound of a latch being released.

'What do you want?' asked a bearded man, raising a paraffin lamp and shining it in the boy's face.

'I'm lost, please help me.'

The man stepped outside, looked around as if to see whether the boy was really on his own, then said, 'Come in.' Heinz crossed the threshold and the man closed the door behind him. The porch smelt of tobacco, and when the boy entered the main living room his eyes began to sting – the air was so thick with smoke that you could have cut it with an axe.

They crossed the room to where seven men were sitting at a large table, staring at Heinz.

On the wall hung a smoke-stained picture of Saint George slaying the dragon.

'What do you want?' asked a long-haired man, who was sitting against the middle of the wall, right under the holy picture.

'Lost, eat. Take pity on me. Eat, frozen,' the boy mumbled in Lithuanian.

'We don't have anything to eat, but here's something to drink,' said the man, pushing a glass of strong alcohol across the table. 'You can't stay here, so drink up and go,' he urged. 'The drink'll stop you from freezing.'

Heinz approached the table, picked up the glass and

emptied it. He coughed. It tasted awful, it burnt his throat and he couldn't breathe. The men watched the boy, not saying anything, and the silence lengthened and became awkward. The man who had let the boy in cuffed him on the shoulder and said, 'Go. Go, you can't stay here, go and forget that you ever saw us.'

Heinz found himself outside again. It was cold, but the alcohol was burning his insides, making him light-headed.

He quickly walked on and on, on and on, wanting to get as far away from the cottage as he could. It was as if his legs moved of their own accord, as if they didn't belong to him, as if they were answerable only to themselves.

Eventually some buildings appeared, and he heard the sound of engines. What looked like car lights were shining straight into his eyes. Heinz could no longer fight off sleep. The world began to spin and he collapsed and fell into a deep slumber.

RENATE WAS WALKING around the small town. She went to the marketplace and saw old Rapolas, who had given her the bread last time.

She asked for bread again, and the old man gave her a thin slice.

Rapolas was quite a strange old man, laughing one moment, frightened the next, then becoming sad. The girl was slightly wary of him, but she had no other choice.

She wanted to go to Lithuania. The old man said he'd take her, and asked her to dance for him.

Renate danced. People were watching, and old Rapolas laughed.

Rapolas's wife, Ona, arrived. Rapolas told her that Renate would be going to Lithuania with them. The old woman liked the girl.

Rapolas, Ona and Renate were in a horse-drawn cart. The old woman was teaching the girl some Lithuanian phrases, and said that from now on her name would be Marytė. The girl was learning to say 'My name is Marytė' in Lithuanian. The old woman explained that it was very important, because soldiers would check whether she was German. Renate tried hard to remember the foreign words.

They came to the bridge over the Nemunas.

The guards stopped them. They asked the girl: 'Aren't you German?'

Renate kept repeating, 'My name is Marytė,' in Lithuanian.

The old man paid the required 'customs duty', but suddenly the alarm clock hidden in the straw went off.

The soldiers discovered the very expensive clock, as well as the other things that had been hidden. They gave the old man a beating, confiscated whatever took their fancy and only then let them go.

After crossing the bridge and travelling on a little further, the old man stopped. He began shouting that this was all Renate's fault, that if it wasn't for her the soldiers wouldn't have stopped them.

He announced that they were in Lithuania, and now that he'd taken her there she should leave them.

Renate climbed down and was left standing in the middle of open fields. But a few moments later the cart halted again; the old woman had apparently talked Rapolas round.

She signalled to Renate, who sprinted back to the wagon.

Renate scrambled back up, and they disappeared into the distance.

Dark. Dark. Dark.

It had been dark for too long. The darkness was complete, and through it came the sound of a woman singing a delightful melody. The words were hard to make out, but it was a mother's song.

Heinz opened his eyes. His hair was stuck to his sweat-covered forehead.

Everything around him was light. He was lying in white sheets.

Heinz saw a woman standing by the window, humming the beautiful song. She was looking through the window, and light was falling through the lace curtains.

Heinz realised that it was his mother. He knew then that everything he had endured had just been a terrible dream.

His lips were dry and he had a fever, but he was smiling, and saying: 'Mama… Mama…'

But then his eyes filled with fear and disappointment – the woman was not his mother, whose face had disappeared and been replaced by that of a stranger.

She was a handsome woman. She smiled gently, but she wasn't his mother.

She was a stranger.

Even the light seemed to change – everything suddenly became greyer, and reality returned. The woman called out something in Russian.

'Aleksey, he's awake, he's awake! The boy's awake!'

Heinz was trying to shout, wanted to shout out his fear and disappointment. He thrashed helplessly in the bed, gripping his pillow.

The woman became frightened. She rushed over to the boy's bed, put her arms around him and tried to calm him down.

She was saying, in Russian, 'There's no need for that. You're ill. There's no need for that, no one's going harm you here.'

A Red Army captain, alarmed by the woman's calls, rushed into the room. He was smartly turned out, with a straight back and a severe, intelligent face: he was probably from an old family of officers.

The woman was his wife, Alyona, a German interpreter. She was expecting a baby, and was already in her eighth month.

Alyona was stroking Heinz's head. Heinz was speaking, but his words weren't coming out right, he didn't seem quite awake yet.

'I haven't done anything wrong, I just want to go home...'

The boy's eyes filled with fear as they met the officer's piercing stare.

'Alyonushka, I told you he was a German!'

'He's a child, just a sick child. Calm down, calm down, my dear boy, it's only Aleksey.'

Alyona hugged Heinz and stroked his head, and Heinz calmed down. He trusted this beautiful and good woman, who so reminded him of his mother.

A SMALL LITHUANIAN town, a street corner, only a few passers-by. It was late afternoon.

Renate was dancing to the unfamiliar melody old Rapolas was playing on a comb. They were selling home-made wicker baskets. The cap at Renate's feet contained just a few small coins.

She had dark circles under her eyes, and her face was dirty. The old man was playing a light, merry tune. No one was buying the wicker baskets he had woven.

An elderly woman came up and stood there for a while, looking pityingly at the dancing girl and the crazy old man. The woman found some coins in her tatty purse and threw them in the cap.

Old Rapolas was happy and smiled, showing his yellow teeth. 'Thank you, dear lady, we will pray for your heart, for your good health. Thank the lady for her generosity! And now, madam, be so kind as to choose a basket, we have both small ones and big ones. I've woven them with my own hands. They can be used for anything – to carry things in, to store things in, and for display.'

The woman picked up the baskets, seeming to be in no hurry to leave.

'Your baskets aren't bad, but what am I going to do with them? There isn't anything to keep in them nowadays.'

She walked off. The old man, livid, turned to Renate.

'Why did I bring you here?' In German, he added: 'Look at them with your sad eyes, offer them the baskets, put them into their hands! You're not doing anything, all you're doing is eating my bread!'

Rapolas smacked Renate lightly on the head, and she quickly drew back so that the old man couldn't reach her, her eyes furious and wild. They stood staring at each other.

'Pick up the baskets, we're going home.'

A long, narrow road, surrounded by snowy fields. Far away the forest loomed and swallowed up the road. The sun was going down and hid behind the forest. It was bright red and promised a cold tomorrow.

Two people were walking along the empty winter road, resembling alien creatures, not of this world: Rapolas and Renate, laden down with the unsold baskets, trod the frozen road as they headed towards the forest.

Renate was lagging a little behind.

They were breathing heavily, rhythmically, exhaling clouds.

Their figures grew smaller and smaller, and eventually vanished in the distance.

RENATE AND RAPOLAS were eating a watery broth. The old woman was unwell and had stayed in bed.

Renate was feeding her with a spoon. She was singing a lullaby that her mother had once sung to her.

Renate brought firewood into the house. Rapolas told her that the old woman, Ona, had died. 'I'm going to invite people over, and you can do whatever you want.'

The old man went out.

RENATE HAD BEEN left alone with the old woman's body. She wasn't particularly afraid of death; after all, she had already seen more than one dead body. But she was afraid of the dark.

And the old man still hadn't come back.

She imagined that she saw shadows and wild animals, that she heard strange sounds – the shutters were banging against the windows, the wind was whistling in the chimney and something howled in the distance.

Renate plucked up her courage, crawled into bed with the dead woman and nestled against her. Humming softly to herself, trying to be brave, she fell asleep.

Renate was dreaming that it was summer and she was with her mother again. A shadow passed over them and she recognised her father, and said 'Papa', but suddenly noticed that her father had no head.

Renate was woken by people coming into the house; she didn't know if they were the ones Rapolas had invited. The people were surprised to see the girl sleeping next to the dead woman.

Renate watched them, and somebody lit a candle.

Rapolas appeared and told Renate to get out of the house. Now that his wife was dead, there was no one to stand up for her.

Renate walked along the empty road, alone.

NIGHT HAD FALLEN over the house where the officer and his wife lived.

Heinz gazed at the stars and the moon, then opened the door to the kitchen, where he rooted around in the dark and found bread, potatoes and other kinds of food. He wanted to steal some, but then thought better of it.

He heard sounds coming from the other room.

He went into the hallway, from where he could see the open bedroom door.

Heinz saw Alyona lying in white sheets, with Aleksey by her side. A gramophone that had come from who knows where sat on the table, playing an old German aria from a comic opera or operetta.

A THAW HAD set in, accompanied by the sound of water dripping from the melting icicles.

Heinz had recovered and was sitting on a bench listening to Alyona, watching military vehicles driving past and soldiers marching down the street. 'It's so wonderful that the war is over,' she was saying. 'My child will be born in peacetime. Just imagine – peace across the whole world. No one will be fighting, no one will be spilling anyone else's blood. Do you really believe that's going to happen?' she asked.

'I need to go home,' said Heinz. 'My mama, my brother Helmut and my sisters are waiting for me. They're starving. I'm afraid they may die.'

'No, they're not going to die; after all, there's peace, everything's going to change now. And we'll pack a lot of food for you. You'll have a full rucksack. And Aleksey will take you to the station, I'll tell him to get you a permit. No one will stop you then.'

They were listening to Mozart, the music that he'd heard at night.

They were sitting outside the house, which had been built very high up on a hill, and were observing the world below. The world was turning on its axis and marching.

ALEKSEY TOOK HEINZ to the station.

He put him on the train, told the driver to make sure that the child got off safely at the right station and, to be on the safe side, handed Heinz a document – the travel permit.

The train started moving. From the expression on the officer's face, it was impossible to tell whether he felt sorry for the boy or was entirely indifferent. Perhaps he hated him, like he did all Germans.

The train chugged through the Lithuanian countryside. Spring was in the air.

THE TRAIN SPEWED smoke and emitted sparks, the huge metal worm groaning as it slowed down and spat out the small boy with his canvas rucksack. He jumped off it onto the icy platform, without waiting for the train to come to a stop. Heinz turned and looked up, but he couldn't see the driver; he was probably busy working the levers to stop the train. He almost collided with some Russian soldiers who had come to meet it, almost tumbled over, his heart beating like a bird that had flown inside him by accident. He didn't stop when someone said something in a language he didn't understand – they were cursing his carelessness. He veered right, and hurried off into the looming darkness.

No one followed him; the soldiers stayed on the crowded platform, and no one asked him anything. Heinz could feel the permit given to him by Aleksey. The writing on it was in Russian, so the boy couldn't read it, but he nevertheless kept it next to his heart – it helped to allay his fears.

The most important thing now was for him to get out of the station. Then he would reach a stream, and things would get easier. He would have to make sure he didn't give himself away, didn't hurry too much or keep glancing around, and avoided people's eyes. People are like wild animals – if you look them in the eye, they'll attack immediately, they won't hesitate. They're like dogs or wolves; you can't look them in the eye, because then they see that you're afraid, they see what's written deep down in your eyes: *Pity me, let me live, don't take my bread away from me, leave me alone, I don't wish you any harm.* And that's the worst thing – the fear in your eyes is like a signal; no one's going to take pity on you, no one's going to pass on the chance to take your bread away from you, the food that was so hard for you to get, food that Mama and Auntie Lotte need, and Renate and Monika, and most importantly Helmut, who for some reason suffered the most when he was hungry. After all, everyone's different – some can bear more than others, but not Helmut. Heinz was listening, trying to hear everything around him and foresee any possible danger, but he couldn't silence his heavy breathing, the wheezing of his lungs and the thumping of his heart; they overpowered everything, all sound – everything.

Suddenly a hand seized him. Heinz leapt back and broke free, and saw a mouth speaking to him and the burning eyes of a sick person – a one-armed person who wanted something from him. His rucksack? His bread? No, not his bread, his mother's bread, Helmut's bread, his sisters' bread. The old man held Heinz in an iron grip, throttling him and trying to tear the rucksack from his back, but the boy bit the horrible, foul-smelling old man, pushed him to the ground and tore himself out of his clutches. He shook himself, hit out at the man, fell down, got up, ran, looked behind him and saw the one-armed man running after him. 'You're my son, you're my son!' yelled the unfortunate man wildly. He was ravaged by hunger, and his voice cut through the night like a scalpel. Heinz heard the word 'son', before diving under a stationary train and emerging a moment later into a brightly lit area guarded by Russians. He heard a shouted order to stop, but he couldn't, the one-armed man was still after him. The madman emerged into the light and stopped as if frozen, great white clouds of breath exploding from his mouth, his eyes filled with fear. 'Stop!' someone shouted, and a shot rang out –

–

–

–

– a bullet whistled past Heinz's head and entered the madman's chest; he was stitched to the night by a round of bullets from an automatic weapon, the word 'son' dying on his lips.

Heinz dived into a ditch, found a hole in a fence and crawled through it like a cat. The barbed wire ripped his cheek and caught hold of his rucksack. The boy scratched his hands as he yanked it off, then he dropped into the black snow and listened. Nothing – only his own breathing and the beating of his heart.

At last the boy calmed down and was able to concentrate; he listened to the night, to the sounds carried on it. The madman had of course stopped chasing him, the soldiers could no longer be heard, no one had set the dogs on him. Somewhere in the distance a shot rang out. He heard words he couldn't understand; perhaps they weren't even words, only the wind coming from the far-away steppes, howling like a wild animal.

Heinz touched his face, and felt blood. His hands were stinging. He dragged the rucksack close to him and fell on his side, felt the damp – the snow was old and wet, the thaw had set in. Hugging the rucksack, he listened again for a moment, and decided to go on. He slowly got up. He mustn't give himself away, he mustn't end up under those lights again – the soldiers guarding the railway station might still be looking for him.

He trudged on. It was easy for him to find his way in the dark, although in places it was hard to know where he was – instead of buildings, there were only piles of bricks and plaster, holes made by bombs dropped from the air. But it wasn't the first time he'd been here, and he could sense where his home was. He was desperate to get home; he knew how eagerly they were waiting for him, he knew what it was like to starve.

Finally he reached the old orchard, or what was left of it. He stopped and listened hard: somewhere in the distance he could hear the enemy's dogs, Alsatians, trained to tear people apart. They were attacking someone, but you couldn't worry about who the victim of those man-eating animals might be when they were so far away. In their yard, all was quiet.

The snow was dirty, making everything even gloomier. The sky was empty; or perhaps there wasn't even a sky – he couldn't see anything except the night.

Heinz walked into the yard. Fear and foreboding made his heart plummet as if into cold water, and a tremor passed through his body. Here was the door to the woodshed, ajar. Could he really have left his mother, his brother and his sisters here? Yes, this was their home. Heinz quietly pushed the door and stepped into the blinding darkness.

Silence.

Inside it was as cold as outside; no one had lit the stove for a long time, no one had boiled water or drunk tea. He couldn't believe that there was no one here, only the night and the mute outlines of things that had been left behind.

'Mama… Mama!' the boy called out in a hoarse voice, as if his mother really might reply, as if she was in this place that had been utterly conquered by the cold, and was only hiding from her son, hiding to tease him, ready to skip out with all the others from their hiding places and welcome him home with shouts of joy. They would hug Heinz, press him to their breasts, kiss his scratched, aching face, light a fire and the candles and cheerfully discuss his adventures, tasting the bread and fatback he'd brought back from Lithuania with delight.

'Mama,' he said to the dark, but the dark was only the dark, it wasn't his mother. At best it was only a refuge and shelter that protected him from drunken soldiers and allowed him to close his eyes and fall into a dream in which he could meet his mother, and everyone else he longed for, but whom he would probably never see again.

Heinz cautiously stepped forward and reached out his hand to touch the iron stove's chimney. It was cold, like everything else around him.

He listened to the silence, as if hoping for an answer, but none came.

His family was no longer here.

He didn't know what had happened to them.

He didn't know where to look for them.

He didn't know what to do.

Throughout his whole time in Lithuania, while he was ill and living with the Russian officer and his wife who translated from German – all that time he had yearned for only one thing: to return home. Especially when Alyona had given him some bread and fatback, when she'd filled his canvas rucksack with the food so desperately needed at home. Especially then.

He'd thought that he'd come back and everything would sort itself out, the cold and starvation would disappear, they'd manage somehow, they'd all go to Lithuania – or perhaps he would return only with his sisters and brother.

After all, Heinz now knew the roads better, he could already speak a little Lithuanian. *We're not going to die, not you, Mama, not my sisters, not Auntie Lotte, not Helmut, who suffers the most when he's starving. Helmut, Helmut, my little brother, you're not going to suffer from starvation any more, I'll look after you, I'll pull you out from the icy jaws of death, and the dogs of hell with their burning eyes will not see us suffering.*

But here he was, sitting in the empty shed, feeling the cold enter his muscles. Exhaustion, despair and fear washed over him.

He had to do something. He threw his rucksack on the ground and found a bundle of matches that had been wrapped in wax paper and rags. He lit a fire, afraid that he'd see his dead sisters with smiles on their faces, that he'd see his mother with her throat cut...

The match ignited, the light penetrated the dense darkness, and— there was no one there. The place was empty. They had left. They had been driven out. They had been taken away. They had escaped. They were somewhere else.

Thank God they weren't in this silence. It was only the silence of an empty dwelling, not a grave.

Heinz lit a fire in the iron stove. The fact that it had been left behind meant that they had been taken away or driven out, because they would never have left such a precious thing behind. It would have been wrong to leave a stove that could protect you from the cold. But perhaps they were too weak, perhaps they hadn't been able to carry a heavy iron stove, for which they would have needed a sled; perhaps they had lost all hope that they would see him again, that Heinz would come back, and had decided to move somewhere else. Perhaps they'd received an offer of a better place in which to live.

The boy watched the crackling fire. He took a loaf of bread from his rucksack. He hesitated a little as he cut off a small piece of the fatback – he couldn't eat much of it, he had to leave some for his family. And if they did return – perhaps not now, not tonight, but perhaps tomorrow – he would know they had been somewhere close, perhaps staying with neighbours. After all, they were waiting for the food he was to bring back home, they were waiting; how could he eat the food without leaving some for his sisters and Helmut? And his mother.

The flame grew. It consumed bits of wood and the legs of an old chair, dancing merrily, as if in another, carefree world where food was plentiful. A place far away, a king's palace replete with shiny silver and silk, where it would be so good to see his sisters, relaxed and happy again—

There was a noise.

Then another.

And another.

Heinz listened, ready to extinguish the fire. He closed the door to the stove to hide the light.

The noise rang out over and over again, sounding like nails being driven into the frozen earth.

The ice on the roof was thawing, dripping.

Heinz smiled: *I lit a fire, and in the world outside all the snow began to melt.*

IN THAT GLOOMY country, the endless forest surrounded the farmsteads and villages like a black wall. The wolves were no longer wary of the humans – they fed on their frozen corpses.

The roadsides were full of them.

Perhaps that was why so many wolves died of rabies. Then again, maybe not – abandoned dogs, too, were food for the wolves.

The sound was long, drawn-out and ghastly. It reawakened your ancient fears, made your skin crawl and ears prick up. Renate's eyes widened in terror; she listened openmouthed to this distant sound, the wild chorus of death.

'Don't be scared, it's only a wolf,' said the boy called Rudolf, who was plucking an old speckled hen.

The bonfire's flames reflected in Renate's eyes. The girl looked over at the forest that surrounded them, at the approaching night. She listened. The flames, soothing and comforting, were licking at a broken piece of metal from a military vehicle they were using as a pot in which to melt snow.

The sharp smell of tobacco reached Renate's nostrils. Rita was smoking a cigarette she'd got from some soldiers or locals. Rita was about thirteen years old. Her hair was tangled, and her eyes both sad and angry. She hardly said a word. Renate was afraid of her. Rudolf was completely different, talkative and cheerful. Strange that the war hadn't made him at all sad, or even aged him. Rita was calmly dragging on the cigarette without coughing, like an old, experienced smoker. You could see experience etched in her face – she had no illusions, she was not afraid of death, she had no great expectations.

The wolf howled again. Perhaps he could smell the blood of the hen, whose belly Rudolf was cutting open with a blunt knife. Renate watched him as he worked, thinking to herself: *Will they give me some of that chicken, or not?* There hadn't been time for the girl to get to know them properly yet. She only knew their names, Rudolf and Rita, and Sparrow – that's how the scrawny and stuttering child had introduced itself. At first, Renate hadn't been able to make out whether it was a boy or a girl. But it was a boy, and they called him Sparrow because he was so small.

Rudolf took whatever was edible out of the fowl; the heart, the liver, some kind of bloody part, and then a strange-looking intestine that reminded her of a bunch of grapes, round yellow pieces of various sizes held together in a bunch.

'What's that?' asked Renate. 'What are those yellow balls?'

'They're eggs.'

'Eggs?'

'Which she was going to lay, this hen. They're tasty, these eggs, they've hardly begun to form.'

'Like children in a woman's belly,' said Rita suddenly. Renate, surprised, turned to look at this morose girl.

'Why?' she asked her.

'D-d-d-don't ask her anything, don't ask her anything,' Sparrow suddenly screamed almost hysterically, 'd-d-don't ask her anything!'

Renate didn't understand and glanced at Rudolf, who was smiling ironically. Smiling and throwing the pieces of chicken into the pot. She remained silent. All she could think about was whether they would give her any chicken or not.

'He's scared,' said Rudolf.

'You could say a child in a woman's belly is also in an egg,' said Rita.

'D-d-don't ask her anything, d-d-don't ask her!' Sparrow screamed again, covering his ears, and he squashed himself into the deepest corner of the shelter they had made from fir branches.

Rudolf laughed. Rita gave him the cigarette butt. He inhaled the acrid smoke, coughed, but continued to smoke.

'We found a murdered woman in a farmhouse. She was naked and they'd sliced open her belly, a tiny baby had fallen out of her belly, it was in a sack like the egg, the sack was split. I suppose the baby had tried to come out, but had frozen. They were both like pieces of ice, the woman and the child.'

Rita said nothing.

Rudolf said: 'I think that's why Sparrow's gone mad. We found him in that house, and when we try to ask him anything about it he only starts screeching. Maybe the woman was his mother. You can try asking him, but he won't answer. He can't hear anything now, he only shakes and his teeth chatter. Rita teases him on purpose. But I think Rita's afraid she could have an egg with a small baby in her own belly; after all, she visits the soldiers.'

'Shut your mouth,' said Rita, and hit him over the head.

The yard was quiet.

It was morning.

Very early in the morning. Dawn was only just breaking.

Heinz opened the door and went out into the morning mist. Water was dripping from the roofs almost as if it were spring — and spring was in fact arriving from somewhere far away, bringing hope with it. Heinz advanced slowly, not knowing what to do or where to go. He suddenly felt lonely, more so than last night; he felt like a snake was pressing on his heart, curling itself around him and squeezing, crushing him. He wanted to shout, to cry, but his eyes were dry, there was only the dampness of an eternal fog on his cheeks — a mist that seemed more like drizzle.

Heinz was walking through his childhood yard. It had been churned up. He walked through the dirty snow, past the broken-down cart, past the well. Through the fog, their old house came into focus. It looked alien, its windows like terrible, blinded eye sockets. Behind those windows, strangers were sleeping. Could this really be the place where his father had punished him, and his mother defended him? Where he'd teased his grandad, because he couldn't stand his tobacco smell, his card-playing, his wine-drinking? Could it really have been there that he had drawn Icarus on a huge sheet of drawing paper for Renate? Could it really be that behind those dead, black eyes they had decorated a Christmas tree with apples and sweets, and angels that his mother and sisters had cut out of paper? Could it really have been here that he and Brigitte had teased each other all the time, and had so eagerly looked forward to their Auntie

Lotte's visits, to the gifts she would bring, and her songs – would he really never again hear his father's sister Lotte singing, with his mama accompanying her on the piano, or his father playing the harmonium? *Punish me, Father, for not knowing, for not appreciating it all, for not rejoicing in every moment of that life, in its smallest things, which make up happiness – punish me, only let me awaken from this dream, only let me wake up from this damp and dead winter, let my eyes be washed with the water of life, let me see things clearly, let everything return to the everyday life of earlier times, let the dreams of demons of death be dispelled... Oh Lord, where should I go now, what should I do?*

Heinz hadn't eaten since last night. In his canvas rucksack he carried everything Alyona had given him for the trip back home: bread, fatback and tinned food from America. But he hadn't been able to eat more than a tiny bit of bread last night, and couldn't bring himself to have anything now. How could he eat this food that had been intended for his mother, his sisters and Helmut? What would be the point of eating now, when he was on his own, when there was no one who would call to him in his mother's voice and hug him? His sisters weren't here for him to laugh at their jokes. So what would be the point when none of them, none who were dear to him, were here and the hope of meeting them was fading with every passing moment? Hope had diminished throughout the night, and now only a weak spark was barely smouldering deep under his heart.

Heinz walked past the fruit trees his father had planted with his own hands. The plums had probably frozen this winter – the buckets of water had been so hard to carry. Here was the Rennet apple tree, under which Mama had once had her photograph taken. A breeze moved her brightly coloured dress, and she was happy and smiling in a now-yellowing photograph. That summer, so easy and yet so hard to remember, lived on in the photograph. He didn't have it any more – it had probably been lost long ago and lay buried somewhere under the debris of war.

Heinz walked slowly, as if on the soundless floor of the sea. Suddenly a silhouette of death loomed out of the mist, the petrified mist of war. No, not a silhouette, a face. With horns, huge and bloody, with foam on its lips and bulging white eyes. It was dead, but it was staring straight at him. It stared and asked: *What are you doing in my realm, what are you doing in this mist? This was your orchard, your yard, your house, but now this is the hell I rule over, the land of the dead, my kingdom.*

Heinz stood frozen to the spot, unexpectedly confronted by the look on the totem's face. He glanced up and could not understand why it had been necessary to place a cow's head on the broken branch of the apple tree – it was heavy, that head, and it was meat, only meat and bone. It was the same as that of any cow, just like the head of their cow, Dusty, who had once fed them, mooing from afar to greet the person coming to milk her. Heinz laughed to himself, answering the totem's reproaches with disdain – he wasn't afraid of this silly masquerade of death, of this mask.

He lowered his eyes and stood silent as the mist settled on his head and shoulders. He closed his eyes, feeling the weight of his exhaustion, the pointlessness of it all and the despair, pressing him into the melting, muddy snow.

He took off his cap and began to cry. He'd thought that he didn't have any tears left, but they burnt like fire, like a blade emerging from the emptiness of an abyss. As if he had woken up.

They weren't tears, but sulphur.

There was no wind, no sound, only the sobbing of a small boy.

But was that really the only sound?

Heinz began to listen, straining to hear – there was a curious noise that wasn't dying away, but growing louder, coming closer, as if a huge worm were crawling along, or water pushing its way through sand.

The boy turned around and saw a large, eerie shadow rise up, drawing nearer, moving rhythmically and threateningly. It was emerging from the fog, from the mist, from a world in which there were no coastlines and no sky.

Finally, he was able to make out shapes – people. A large group of people with their hands down by their sides, feet dragging along the road that led past the yard, moving in step, slowly, impelling itself forward from one edge of the mist to the other. To where? Who knows... They looked like they had died a long time ago. Heinz was frightened that the death mask was right – he had died a long time ago, as had these skeletons passing by.

A living person came running out of the column led by several lightly armed Russian soldiers (they weren't about to let anyone escape). Yes, a living person, a living person was running towards him joyfully, paying no attention to the Russian shouting at him – shouting more from duty than any real concern. The person was calling his name: 'Heinz, Heinz, it's me, Albert, I was looking for you, I knew we'd be passing your house!' They embraced for a brief moment, clapped each other on the back. 'I can't find my family, and yours are no longer here, they were probably driven out. I have to go, but perhaps we'll find them again. We must find them again. They say we're being taken to Germany, they're sending us to Germany. We'll find them there. After all, we can't be lost in the world for ever – we can't, and even if we do get lost we'll try to find each other, we must try. Let's go now. Our people are long gone, and what can we do on our own? They won't let us stay here alone.'

Suddenly reality returned and the gravel crunched loudly under the feet of the Germans being driven forward. There were old people, women, children, some carrying a bundle, some a piece of furniture, others nothing at all. Albert looked gaunt; there were dark circles under his eyes, but they were alive and shining. He was saying: 'What a joy to have found you! I never believed it possible, but all the same I tried looking into your house from a distance, in case by chance, in case...and suddenly I saw someone standing by the apple tree, and I thought: "That could be Heinz." Heinz, I could see it was really you – God, I'm so pleased to have found you!'

One of the Russian soldiers shouted something, the column had almost passed, they had to go on, they had to.

The boys joined the line and disappeared into the mist. Heinz looked back a couple of times, but there was nothing to see.

A COVERED LORRY carrying supplies approached a shop in the square of a small town.

Three boys and Renate were waiting for the right moment.

As the lorry drove past the shop, the driver beeped his horn. He turned into the yard at the back and stopped by the delivery entrance.

Stasė, the shop assistant, came to meet the driver. Stasė signed the delivery note, and then she and the driver began loading trays of bread. The black loaves were all the same shape, and did not look very appetising.

'The bread's always only half-baked now,' said Stasė with a sigh.

She and the driver disappeared into the storeroom.

The children were watching everything from around the corner.

'Let's go...now!' shouted Rudolf.

Renate hesitated a little, but then ran to the vehicle with the others. They went to where the bread was, and each of them grabbed what they could.

The driver appeared from the shop, yelling at them, and took off his belt as he ran.

'I'll show you, you damned thieves! The devil take you!' he shouted angrily.

The children ran off in different directions. Renate was the last to get away; she didn't know what to do. She was holding a roll pressed to her chest. Her foot slipped and she fell flat on her face.

The driver grabbed the girl by the scruff of her neck as if

she were a dog, shook her vigorously and started whipping her with the belt. Renate cried out, frightened, ashamed and in pain.

The driver's face was bright red from rage; he kept beating her and beating her, not caring where the blows landed.

The shop assistant ran out of the storeroom and grabbed the driver's arm.

'Stop it, stop it, for God's sake!'

'She's a thief, a damned thief!'

'She's just a child, a child! Let go of her, don't hit her, let her go!'

'They're everywhere now, like lice!'

Renate was lying on her back now. The bread had rolled out of her hands. Her eyes were full of fury and fear as she looked up at the woman who was speaking in a language she didn't understand.

Renate crawled painfully forward to reach the roll. She grabbed hold of it, determined not to let anyone take it away from her.

'They need to be beaten while they're still young, or it'll be too late when they're older... Can't you see how she's looking at us?'

Stasė asked Renate: 'Where are you from? Who's your mother? You don't need to be afraid of me. Why are you stealing? It's not right to steal, it's not right to steal.'

The driver picked up another tray.

'She's a German, one of those wolf-children – the area around the forest is full of them. They're like lice, they steal anything, they're always begging.'

Stasė asked her, in German: 'Are you German? Can you understand me?'

Renate nodded.

'Don't be scared of me, don't run off. But you shouldn't steal. Are you hungry?'

Renate nodded.

The driver looked at them and laughed, as if to say, *What can you do with these women?* He spat, got into the lorry and shouted: 'The delivery note is on the box!'

With some difficulty, the lorry edged out of the potholed yard.

'Where's your mama?' asked Stasė.

'I've lost her…'

The woman regarded the frightened, beaten little girl and felt a pang in her chest.

'You poor thing.'

Renate looked at Stasė. Perhaps she was beginning to trust this young woman.

Stasė gave her an encouraging smile.

STASĖ SOLD BREAD and other basic foodstuffs. The women who came to her always complained about the winter, about being hungry, about the quality of the bread, about the awful times they were living in.

Renate was sitting in the corner of the office. The door that led through to the shop was slightly ajar, and Renate could hear them talking in a language she didn't understand, and saw Stasė working hard behind the counter. She kept looking over at Renate and smiling reassuringly.

Renate had lost count of the rolls she'd had. She took a bite from another; she struggled to get it down, but pushed the piece deep into her mouth with her finger and swallowed.

A louse crawled across the girl's face.

STASĖ'S HOUSE WAS divided into two. Stasė, her husband and her sister lived in one part, while the other housed several members of the NKVD-controlled paramilitary units tasked with hunting down Lithuanian anti-Soviet partisans, from whom came an endless stream of drunken singing and swearing.

A small, unprepossessing local Russian called Mikita came weaving through the yard. He had signed up to be one of the *stribai*, 'exterminators', as they were called. He went over to a window from which the sound of laughter and inebriated voices came, and knocked on it. He squatted, so that he couldn't be seen, and laughed as he did so. The men inside fell silent. One of them warily looked through the window, and Mikita sprang up so that they were now face-to-face. The man disappeared, and Mikita laughed again.

A drunken exterminator came out of the house, incensed.

'Fuck it, Mikita, you'll get it one day! I'm going to shoot you, see if I don't!'

'Who're you afraid of? You're afraid of me, Mikita. Everyone's afraid of Mikita now. Go on being afraid, fuck you.'

'Like I'm going to be afraid of you. Did you bring us some of that homemade alcohol?'

The exterminator spread his legs wide, stumbled a little, and then pissed right against the wall of the house.

RENATE WAS SITTING in a barrel of warm water, surrounded by soap bubbles and rising steam.

She could hear Mikita and the other exterminators' drunken shouts as they scuffled in the porch.

Stasė was bathing the girl. She thoroughly soaped her hair.

Elzė was looking through the window into the yard, where a drunken man with a rifle was staggering around. Elzė was Stasė's older sister, a spinster who always looked angry and dissatisfied. She never smiled, as if she was trying to hide rotting teeth. But she couldn't stop talking.

Stasė was frightened by the exterminators' shouts, but tried not to show it. Elzė carried on talking.

'Why did you bring that German girl home? Don't you know they have to be registered at the local council? These German children, they come here begging, stealing, spreading diseases – they're death, and with these Russians in our house, these exterminators always walking around drunk, do you want us to be deported, to be sent off to Siberia? Why do you need this girl? Why do you need her, now that you're married, when you have a man, when you're going to have children of your own? Are you prepared to go to Siberia because of her? Do you want me to be deported to Siberia because of you, because of your kindness, because of this girl who you can only talk to in whispers, so that no one can hear you speaking German?'

Stasė wrapped Renate in a large towel, lifted her out of the barrel and started to dry her. In Lithuanian, she said to the girl: 'It's just as well you can't understand anything my bad-tempered sister is babbling on about.'

Stasė took Renate into the living room, where a bed had been made ready.

'I'm going to lend you a nightgown.' She laughed. 'It's mine, so it's going to be too big for you. But tomorrow I'm going to sew you a beautiful new one, and a dress. But now you need to sleep.'

Stasė took her nightgown from the wardrobe. Standing Renate on a chair, she pulled it over her head, then laid her down in the bed made up with fresh white linen. She sat on the edge of the bed and stroked the girl's head.

Renate stretched her arms out towards Stasė.

Stasė lay down next to the child.

Renate suddenly hugged her with all her might.

'Be my mother, be my mother!'

'I will be, I promise,' Stasė said gently, and kissed the child's head.

Renate's eyes closed.

Stasė's husband Antanas was chopping wood. The sound echoed in the clear morning silence. Smoke was rising from the chimney, straight up into the sky.

Renate woke up to the early-morning light streaming in through the window. She could hear the sound of Antanas's axe.

She stared up at the ceiling for a while, as if not believing her own eyes, then quickly threw off the blanket, got up and walked barefoot across the gleaming, clean floor.

There was a noise coming through the half-open door to the kitchen. She moved towards it, and saw that Stasė was sewing a dress. She looked happy. Renate wanted to commit Stasė's face, this moment, to memory. Perhaps that way she could understand people better.

The clock on the wall was ticking loudly. Renate stepped back from the door and looked around the room in which she had been sleeping. She walked over to the clock and inspected the pendulum, then the old sideboard, the delicate porcelain ballerina and a portrait in a metal frame of a beautiful smiling woman who looked like Stasė.

The girl picked up the ballerina and studied her, entranced, but when she was about to put her back down a sound from the kitchen made her jump. The ballerina fell to the floor and, to the girl's horror, broke. At that moment, the door opened.

Renate was frightened, and quickly dived back into bed.

She looked timidly at Stasė, who was holding a dress and some sort of coat or sheepskin.

'Good morning! Did I startle you? Don't be scared.'

Stasė carefully pulled back the blanket, held her arms out to Renate, hugged her and stood her again on the chair.

'I've made this for you, try it on.'

Stasė put the dress on Renate.

'You have to look nice, we're going to introduce you to your papa.'

Renate, whose head had just emerged through the neck of the dress, became anxious. To her papa?

'Yes. His name is Antanas. You'll need to learn a few words of Lithuanian. All right?'

Renate nodded.

Stasė took Renate outside, where Antanas was chopping wood. She had dressed the girl in a coat that was slightly too big for her.

Antanas stood there holding the axe, and considered the girl. To Renate, he seemed like a giant.

Stasė said, in Lithuanian: 'We have something to show you.' She bent down and, smiling mischievously, told Renate: 'Ask him the question, darling.'

Renate spoke shyly, carefully pronouncing each syllable of Lithuanian: 'Papa, do you have fleas?'

Antanas was stunned into silence, then erupted with a thunderous laugh.

Renate wasn't sure how to react. She looked at Stasė, who said, 'Good girl!' and smiled contentedly.

Antanas, seeing that he might have frightened the girl, knelt down beside her.

Renate snuggled up to Stasė, as if trying to hide.

Antanas smiled. 'No, I don't have fleas – dear daughter.' He put his hand out and took Renate's hand.

'You need some gloves. What's the German for "gloves"?'

'We have gloves,' said Stasė, and gave Renate some patterned mittens that she had knitted herself. They were her own; she would knit another pair for herself, she wasn't cold today. 'I didn't have time to knit a new pair. I'll do it when I come home from work.'

'Put Stasė's gloves on.' He tried to help Renate into them with one hand, and Stasė rushed to help. The girl could now see that this tall, broad-shouldered man had only one arm.

'Are you going to help me chop wood?'

'Don't joke, Antanas. How can she help you, she's still just a child.'

'Don't worry, we'll work it out, you'll see.'

Stasė shook her head reproachfully, looking Antanas in the eye, as if to say, *Don't talk such nonsense*, but Antanas smiled and said, 'Don't worry.'

Stasė squatted beside Renate, pushed a wayward curl under the girl's headscarf and said in German: 'I have to go to work. You stay here with Papa.'

Renate looked at her with apprehension in her eyes.

Stasė kissed Renate and left. She disappeared along the path that led to the small town.

Antanas spoke a very funny German, mispronouncing words and dropping in the occasional word of Lithuanian, explaining certain things with gestures.

'You're going to help me chop wood, all right?'

Renate looked at him and said nothing.

'Don't be afraid, it's not hard. You show me which piece of wood I need to chop. Which one? You choose. Don't be afraid, my dear. Well, which one should I chop?'

At last Renate plucked up her courage and pointed to a piece of wood. Her father took it, cut into it with his axe, put it on another, bigger log, pulled the axe out, raised it and split the wood with one blow.

MIKITA EMERGED FROM the exterminators' part of the house, still half-asleep. He took out a cigarette, lit it and looked at the bright winter morning, a rifle hanging from his shoulder.

He saw Antanas chopping wood at the end of the yard by the barn, and next to him Renate, who was showing him which piece of wood to chop next.

Mikita blew steam and smoke from his mouth.

Antanas was cheerfully chopping the wood. He was strong, it was easy, the pile was growing.

Renate was rolling a large snow-covered log along the ground.

Antanas laughed: 'I can split that in one blow, get me a heavier one.'

Renate smiled, no longer afraid of this large man with an axe.

They were surprised when hunchbacked Mikita came over.

'Why aren't you at work?'

Renate flinched. Frightened, she stared at the hunchback.

People normally start by greeting one another – even a pig will oink. 'Where did you get the wood from? Who allowed you to chop it?'

'It's from my father's forest,' said Antanas.

'All the forests now belong to the state,' said Mikita, and gave Renate a strange look. She moved closer to the wall of the hay barn.

'The forester let me have some wood from trees that had fallen down,' said Antanas.

'Who are you?' Mikita asked Renate.

She didn't reply.

'I think she's a German.'

'She's not a German, she's my wife's sister's daughter from Kaunas. There's hardly any food left in the town…'

'And *I* think she's a German,' Mikita said in Russian. He looked at the girl. 'Why aren't you saying anything? Why are you looking at me like that?'

'Don't frighten her, you can see the child is afraid of strangers.'

'You're German, yes? What's your name? What's your name? Are you German?'

In a clear voice, Renate answered him in Lithuanian: 'My name is Marytė. My name is Marytė.'

'You see, her name's Marytė, I told you.'

Mikita stared at Renate for a while, smiled crookedly, spat, and walked off in the direction of town.

ANTANAS, RENATE AND Elzė were having lunch. Elzė was serving the soup, and Antanas was sitting at the end of the table, slicing the bread. Renate was waiting to eat, spoon in hand.

'Give Marytė some more, she's such a good worker,' said Antanas, smiling.

Elzė placed a full bowl of soup in front of her. She smiled at Renate, but didn't say any loving words. Renate ate hungrily, listening attentively to the language she didn't understand, and observing the adults.

'These times we're living in, God, there's shooting every night! They say people are being deported again, they come in the night and take them away. We've got Russkies on the other side of our wall, and Mikita, the hunchback, is here every day... The smallest thing and we'll be living in Siberia, I said to Stasė yesterday and I'm saying to you now, we can't do this. We can't – we have to protect ourselves, to think of ourselves, not take in foreign children. There are children everywhere, Germans and Russians, and our own too, it's not as if you can look after all of them. We have to look after ourselves now, ourselves.'

ANTANAS AND STASĖ were making love; they were young, and beautiful in their passion for each other.

There was a noise from the kitchen; a pot fell, a bucket was knocked over.

Renate had collapsed in the kitchen. She felt nauseous, she vomited.

Stasė cleaned the girl up. She blew on the embers in the stove and said she'd make some chamomile tea right away.

Elzė also appeared, woken by the noise. She said: 'You see, the German girl is unwell, we'll catch something from her.'

Antanas angrily told Elzė to go back to sleep. He picked up Renate, who was still sobbing, and carried her around the kitchen.

'Don't cry, don't cry. Do you have a tummy ache? Are you afraid of something, did you have a bad dream?'

He carried the girl to the window, where he showed her the full moon and told her that the moon laughs at people who don't sleep at night.

Renate wrapped her arms around Antanas and pressed her cheek against his shoulder, calm now. She finally felt safe.

Stasė gave her a cup of chamomile tea and told her to drink it.

At that moment, shots were fired. It sounded like people were shooting at one another at the edge of the forest.

'Oh God, there's shooting…blow out the lamp!'

'Those damned exterminators!'

'Come here, my little one,' said Stase, 'let's go to bed.'

She then said to Antanas: 'We don't want her getting even more frightened.'

153

Antanas blew out the paraffin lamp and remained standing there, looking in the direction of the shots. Several bullets flew past, close to the house.

The shots became less frequent.

THE PATH FROM the house went downhill and was very slippery.

Stasė was taking Renate into town. Antanas scattered gravel on the ground, so that his 'ladies' wouldn't slip and fall. Stasė laughed.

Antanas embraced Stasė and kissed her.

He crouched down beside Renate and gave her a peck on the cheek.

'Be careful, don't slip.'

Renate and Stasė went on their way.

STASĖ AND RENATE were walking along the edge of the forest in the direction of town. Stasė was holding Renate's hand. White clouds were coming out of their mouths – it was freezing cold.

There was a noise behind them. They turned.

A horse-drawn cart caught up with them, and then overtook them. A couple of severe-looking men were walking next to the cart in silence. They frightened Renate – they were looking straight at her.

Stasė hugged Renate to her as they stood aside and watched the cart go past. Someone was lying inside it, covered with straw.

As it went past it left a red trail. It was blood. It was carrying the bodies of forest brothers – as the Lithuanians called the anti-Soviet partisans – who had been killed. The exterminators were taking them into town.

A hand was poking out through the straw.

THE TRAVELLING DOCTOR'S assistant finished examining Renate.

'It's nothing serious, she's just weak. The vomiting might have been from overeating, perhaps the food was too rich for her. The girl needs to have some calf's liver and milk to strengthen her blood.'

'Calf's liver?'

'I know you can hardly get it now, but if you were able to, just boil it and give it to her to eat.'

'I'll get some, somehow.'

'And why are you so sad, Marytė? You need to smile.'

'She does smile, my child does smile,' said Stasė.

'You're brave people, my dear Stasė.' She turned to the girl. 'You, Marytė, should smile more, then people will be nicer to you – why is she looking at me so angrily?'

'You're imagining it, Anelė – she's a very good child, we just need some documents for her. She doesn't have anything to show she's Lithuanian. We need to send her to school.'

'The first thing you have to do is teach her to speak Lithuanian well. As for the documents, all I can do is issue her a medical card, but that's not enough. Perhaps the priest can help you.'

'At least issue a card for her, at least that – do whatever you can. Thank you, thank you.'

STASĖ WENT TO the dresser, unlocked one of the drawers and took out a delicate little box.

She took the box to the table, unlocked and opened it. There was all kinds of jewellery inside, some letters from her sister and the porcelain ballerina that Renate had broken.

Stasė asked Renate to come closer. She took out some gold earrings, put them on and looked in the mirror inside the box. 'These earrings were my mother's,' she said to the girl.

'That dancer…it broke—' said Renate.

'It's not important, she was only standing on one leg, and I've been saying for a long time that she's going to lose her balance one day. She should be thrown out.'

Renate picked up a beautiful locket and examined it.

'Open it, there's something inside.'

Renate opened the locket and saw a photograph of a small girl.

'That's my sister Onutė, she was a very pretty girl. She gave me this locket to remember her by. As if I could ever forget her. She lives in Kaunas now. She's a dancer. We went to see her dancing with my father, who's dead now. She was very beautiful, with a full white skirt. My father cried while he watched her.'

Renate picked up a photograph of a woman who looked like Stasė.

'Is this her?'

'Yes, that's her, you can see how that small girl has grown into a young woman. She looks a lot like Elzė.'

———

Elzė had been standing in the doorway for a long time.

'Yes, show her everything – the necklaces, earrings, show her – then she can steal them.'

Stasė took off the earrings and wrapped them in a small handkerchief. She didn't put them away again, but left them on the table. She locked the box and put it back in the drawer.

As Elzė walked past Stasė, she said, 'Yes, take everything, sell it…'

'They're my earrings, not yours,' said Stasė.

Renate was left alone in the room. Stasė's and Elzė's unintelligible voices could be heard coming from the kitchen. Through the window, Renate saw Stasė hurrying off somewhere.

Renate looked at the photographs on the dresser but didn't touch anything, afraid that she might break something else.

She walked around the living room and stopped by the photograph of a man, probably Stasė's father. The elderly, whiskered man was dressed in hunting clothes, holding a rifle, a large and clever-looking dog at his side.

Renate stared at the image of Jesus Christ hanging on the wall. He seemed to be smiling almost imperceptibly, and pointing to his heart, his forehead pierced by a crown of thorns.

She looked at him for so long that Christ suddenly seemed to wink at her playfully.

Renate couldn't believe it. She waited for Christ to give her another sign – but a picture is just a picture.

Elzė came in, startling the girl.

'Come with me, I'll give you something nice to eat,' she said.

Elzė was smiling pleasantly at her, but her eyes frightened the girl.

Elzė had put some sliced bread out on the table. She wiped a dusty glass jar with jam in it, opened it, placed it next to the bread, gave Renate a spoon and poured out some tea for her.

Elzė was speaking almost like a beguiling witch: 'I made this jam myself, I picked the berries myself last summer. Stasė also made some, but they've finished it – she and Antanas don't know how to save. They eat everything, they give everything to other people, while I put things aside and hold on to them. My sister and her husband are very good people, but they still don't know what saving for a rainy day means. Do you know where Stasė's gone now? She's gone to sell the earrings her dead mother gave her as a present, because she wants to give you calf's liver. They hardly have anything to eat themselves, but they want to give you everything. And what's going to happen when she no longer has any earrings and everything's been eaten? What's she going to sell then? You're a very good girl, very pretty, and I like you very much, but they don't understand that they can't support you. You need to go home to your mother, your real mother, who misses you very much, who's waiting for you, who's got some presents waiting for you when you get home. Eat the jam, eat up.'

Renate very much wanted the jam, but tried to eat as little of it as possible.

'You probably don't know,' said Elzė, 'and Stasė and Antanas won't tell you, since they don't want to let you go – they like you like a beautiful toy, a doll – but quite nearby, just on the other side of the forest, the Russians have gathered a lot of Germans. I heard that your mama could be there too. Stasė and Antanas are good people, but they're a little bit selfish, and what's going to happen when a stork brings them a baby? They won't need you any more, and in the meantime your mama, who's been looking for you and hasn't found you, may have left already and never come back. If you stay on, no one will need you and you'll be lonely. I can take you through the forest, to your mother. Eat the jam, eat up.'

Renate was looking at Elzė, uncertain whether to believe what this strange, smiling woman was saying to her.

Renate's lips were covered with jam, blood-red.

'Do you want me to take you to your mama?'

IT WAS QUIET in the forest; not even the smallest branch was moving, everything was covered with a thick layer of snow.

Then came the sound of snow crunching underfoot, and Elzė and Renate appeared.

Renate kept falling behind, and Elzė waited for her to catch up.

'It's not far, not at all far to go now, we've nearly reached the edge of the forest.'

They walked for a long while, with Renate struggling to keep up. The forest became denser; it was slowly getting dark.

Renate stopped. Elzė turned around. She had a sly smile on her face.

'Let's go. Why have you stopped? Don't you want to be with your mama? Your mama's waiting for you.'

And then Renate sensed something cold coming from Elzė's mouth, as if it were the wind and emptiness. The tops of the trees in the forest began to rustle, the snow began to fall from the snow-covered firs. 'It's not far now,' said the witch, spinning on one foot. A raging snowstorm was spewing from her mouth, a snowstorm that covered everything; everything around them was white, and the trees swayed like the masts on a sailing ship in the middle of an endless, wild sea of ice.

Elzė reached out her hand and advanced upon Renate. She came closer and closer.

All of a sudden, the distant howling of a wolf cut through the whistling snowstorm and the approaching dark of the night. It seemed to wake the girl up. Renate began running, the snowstorm raging all around her, the trees and their shadows, the snow and Elzė all part of the same maelstrom.

Renate ran and ran, chased by the witch's laughter.

RENATE WAS TOSSING and turning in bed. Finally she opened her eyes. She was drenched in sweat. She had a fever.

Renate could hear Stasė and Elzė talking in the kitchen. Stasė was scolding Elzė for letting Renate catch a cold.

Renate calmed down. She stared at the ceiling and saw her mother, her brothers, her sisters – and someone else, whose face she could no longer remember. Her father.

Renate clutched her pillow tightly, and wept.

THE DAYS PASSED by quickly and happily. Scents soaked the air like a drink sweetened with honey, or the sap from a tree, which in spring comes up from the very depths of the earth and flows along the branches until it rises towards the sun, making buds burst and blossoms bloom. In those buds, in their power, you can feel the fruit, its sourness and coolness, lightly refreshing the palate.

The days passed in this way, one after another.

RENATE CAME OUT of the woodshed carrying a bundle of firewood. Her attention was caught by the icicles hanging down from the roof of the shed – there were a lot of them. They looked like dragons' teeth.

Renate dropped the wood and looked at the icicles. She touched one of them, then raised her eyes and looked at the clouds.

She picked up a piece of wood and merrily began hitting the icicles, until they broke with a light tinkling sound.

Mikita, half drunk, emerged from somewhere, scaring the girl.

'And what are you doing here?' he asked her in Russian.

She let out a gasp. Frightened, she turned around and looked at Mikita, still holding the piece of wood in her hand.

'What are you doing here? Tell me, who are you? You're German, aren't you? Say "Heil Hitler!" Say "Heil Hitler!" Do you hear me? You're a German.'

'My name is Marytė,' Renate said in Lithuanian.

'I know you're German. I could shoot you. I have a gun, I could shoot you.'

'My name is Marytė.'

'No, you're a German. Say "Heil Hitler!"'

Mikita was holding the girl by her neck, a pistol in his other hand. His eyes were bloodshot. Renate couldn't breathe, but hoarsely repeated the same phrase: 'My name is Marytė.'

Antanas came running across the yard. He reached the exterminator and the girl, grabbed hold of Mikita and pulled the child away from him, took away Mikita's pistol and pushed him against the stack of firewood, where the icicles were hanging down.

'What do you want from the girl? What do you want, you animal? Didn't my father help you enough? You worked for him, you had a good life, didn't we help you enough? Say something, you animal…say something!' Antanas shouted, still holding on to Mikita.

'I was only joking, I just wanted to have a laugh, Antanas. I didn't want to—'

'If you touch my child again, I'll kill you.'

Antanas took the bullets out of the pistol and flung them into the snow, then threw the pistol at Mikita.

'Don't be afraid,' said Antanas, 'don't be afraid, my dear little daughter, he won't touch you, he won't touch you again. Let's go inside.'

They went off, Mikita watching them go. It looked as though he was crying drunken tears.

ANTANAS WAS SITTING on the bench, watching the wood burning in the stove. Stasė was sitting next to her husband, her arms around him and her head on his shoulder as he talked.

'We have to follow the doctor's advice, we have to see the priest, perhaps we'll be able to get the right documents for the girl somehow. It's becoming dangerous. That Mikita is a coward and a shit, but he really frightened the child, and what if it hadn't been Mikita but someone else...the poor child. We have to take some fatback to the priest, and that last jar of honey – we have no choice, we need those documents.'

'Yes, my dear Antanas, yes...'

Stasė kissed Antanas.

'There's no need for that, my dearest Stasė. The child's watching.'

Renate was standing in the doorway. A look of surprise flashed across her face when Antanas mentioned her, then she turned around and left the room. Stasė and Antanas laughed softly.

Stasė was walking through the town square with the girl. A drunk exterminator was walking about, watching everyone as he guarded the mutilated corpses of partisans that had been exhibited in the square.

Stasė covered the girl's eyes with her hand to stop her from seeing the horrific display.

'Why are you doing that? Let her see the bandits,' said the exterminator.

Stasė didn't reply, but walked on, trying to protect her daughter from the sight.

The woman and the girl went into the church, where Stasė knelt and crossed herself. She sat Renate down in a pew. 'Wait for me here, my dear little daughter, I'll be back soon. I have to go to the sacristy.'

The church was almost empty.

Renate sat in the pew, waiting. She looked at the huge Christ above the altar, at the angels and the saints. She silently began to pray.

God, help us all to be safe, so that no one dies for no reason, so that everyone finds their families and has enough to eat. Help us never to be afraid...

Christ smiled silently, looking down with compassion.

A little while later Stasė came back, took Renate by the hand and led her into the sacristy. The priest was sitting there. He was a portly man, with a good-natured face and red cheeks.

He turned around when Stasė and Renate entered the sacristy.

'So this is our poor lost little girl... What's your name, my child?'

'My name is Marytė,' said the frightened girl, in Lithuanian.

'You see what a clever girl she is, what a clever girl is our Marytė,' said the priest, and laughed.

He looked at her for some time without speaking, but his eyes smiled. Renate decided that he must be a good person.

Antanas and Stasė were lying in bed, but weren't asleep yet.

'The priest asked: "Do you believe in Jesus Christ?" And she answered: "I do."'

'A clever girl…'

'He then asked: "Are you a Catholic?" And she just looked at him and didn't say anything.'

'How can the child be expected to know if she's a Catholic, a member of the Reformed Church or some other faith?'

'The priest then said, "We have to baptise you – it'll do no harm if it's for a second time."'

'We have to have her baptised, and then we'll have the documents we need.'

'The priest said that she would be entered into the register of deaths, then the entry would have to be deleted, with the explanation that an error had been made.'

'If that's what the priest said, it means he knows what he's talking about. Everything should be fine now— Did you hear that?'

They listened carefully.

They could now hear the sound clearly – someone was knocking on the window.

Antanas went from the bedroom into the kitchen, and over to the window. The knocking came again.

'Who's there? What do you want? What's going on?'

'It's me, Mikita. Open up. We need to talk, open up.'

Stasė appeared in the doorway.

Elzė also came out of her room.

Antanas went into the porch, unbolted the door, let Mikita in and took him into the kitchen.

'You have to run, get your things together and run – they're going to deport you tonight.'

'Oh Jesus,' said Stasė. She quietly, almost automatically, began to pray.

'Someone reported you because of the German girl… It wasn't me, honest, it wasn't me.'

Antanas turned to Stasė, unsure what to do. His glance fell on Elzė, who seemed neither surprised nor frightened.

'Antanas, it wasn't me! Just hurry,' said Mikita again. He hurried back to the porch and disappeared into the night.

'What's going to happen now, oh Jesus, what's going to happen now?'

Through the window they saw vehicle lights coming towards their farmstead from the edge of the forest.

'That's it. They're coming. Get the child up, get our warm clothes, the bedding, and I'll bring down the fatback from the attic. We have to get ready.'

Stasė saw Renate standing in the doorway, frightened. She hugged her and began to sob.

'They're going to take us away, they're going to take us away, my dear child, my dear child, what's going to become of us—'

'Shh! Stasė, get the child, get ready, those devils aren't going to wait,' her husband interrupted sternly. He threw on his jacket, and quickly went up to the attic to get the fatback.

'I told you they would take you away because of this devil's daughter. I told you!' Elzė said angrily.

'Shut your mouth, you heartless thing! I'm not going to allow an innocent child to suffer. Get ready, Marytė.'

Stasė hurried into the other room.

Renate stood there watching them rush around, eyes full of fear.

Antanas hurried in and put the fatback on the table. Stasė brought Renate her coat and a knitted jumper.

'You have to hurry, my dear child, run as far away as you can, far away so they won't catch you. Go to the doctor, to my friend Anelė – she'll help you. You remember where it is? It's where you were weighed. Remember?'

Renate nodded.

The vehicle lights shone through the windows. They heard steps, voices, then someone banged on the door.

Stasė took Renate into the other room.

Antanas called out: 'Who's that? Wait a moment, I'm just putting on some clothes!'

Stasė ran to fetch something, while blows rained down on the door. She brought back the locket with her sister's portrait and a small cross in it, and gave it to Renate.

Stasė kissed Renate, made the sign of the cross over her, then opened the small window, helped the girl to slip through it and, crying, called after the girl: 'Run, my dear little daughter, run, may God help you! And remember me, remember me and Antanas…'

Renate was scared; there was a lot of noise outside, cars droning. She fell over in the snow, but quickly got up and ran, ran without stopping.

Stasė went into the kitchen. The exterminators were already in the house. Their leader was a large man with a red face.

'Where's the German girl?' asked the leader.

'What German girl?' asked Antanas, feigning ignorance.

'Fuck it, Antanas, I'm not joking around – where's the girl? Tell me or you'll soon be spitting blood.'

'Girl? Do you mean Stasė's sister's daughter?'

'Daughter? All right, where's this daughter?'

'We put her in a car to Kaunas.'

The leader of the exterminators suddenly hit Antanas with the butt of his gun. 'What the fuck are you babbling about – "we put her in a car"? Search the house!' he ordered the exterminators.

Two of them rushed off to check the rooms. Stasė huddled up to Antanas, whose lip was bleeding.

Renate ran through the forest. She kept tripping over fallen branches, slipping over in the snow and lying there for a moment, listening, then getting up and running again.

The exterminators' lorry was parked in the yard. Next to it there were several of them, armed. Antanas and Stasė came out of the house, put their bundles into the vehicle, climbed into the trailer and stood hugging one another tightly.

A scream could be heard – it was Elzė.

She was in the doorway; she didn't want to go anywhere.

The leader of the exterminators kicked her hard in the bottom and she fell off the step into the yard, onto her face.

'Get up, you bitch, stop blubbering!'

Elzė tried to stand up, crawled over to the leader and kissed his feet, sobbing loudly.

'I'm innocent, I'm innocent! I didn't take that German girl in, it wasn't me! Why should I be sent to Siberia, sir? Why me? I'm innocent, I said the girl was a German, I said that she should be thrown out, I told them, it wasn't me who brought her home, sir, have mercy on me, have mercy on me! I was the one who told you about it, I didn't do anything, I know they have to be registered, those Germans!'

A blow from the butt of the gun to Elzė's face silenced her; she fell to the ground without a sound, her face bloody.

Antanas jumped out of the trailer, lifted Elzė up and helped her to get in. Elzė had partly recovered now and began sobbing, but quietly, knowing it was hopeless.

Stasė put her arms around Elzė and gently wiped her bloody face. They were sitting in a corner of the trailer, all three pressed closely against each other.

The lorry moved off and left the village behind.

The figures of Stasė, Elzė and Antanas faded into the distance; it became impossible to make them out any longer. The lorry turned into a narrow track. Only its lights could still be seen.

Renate was making her way through the forest. She could hear the sound of the lorry and see its headlights shining through the trees.

It was the same kind of lorry that was deporting Stasė and Antanas, but it might not have been the exact same one.

Renate watched the battered lorry as it passed by, clattering and clanging. There was nothing in her eyes – neither fear, nor anger.

It was early morning. A small figure appeared at the end of a street in town – it was Renate. She was not sure of her way, but finally she seemed to recognise something and turned in the direction of the house where the doctor's assistant's surgery was.

Renate knocked on the door.

Anelė opened it, and asked in a frightened voice: 'What's happened?'

'I'm Marytė. The exterminators have taken my Mama Stasė to Siberia, they've also taken away my Papa Antanas.'

The doctor's assistant understood Renate's words and grew even more frightened. 'Oh God, they've taken my dearest Stasė away, oh God, they've taken Stasė away.'

'They told me to come here, they said you'd help…'

'I told her they shouldn't take you in, I told her you were death, that you were bad luck, a walking misfortune! Go away, get away from here, go somewhere else, look for another home, I can't— I won't take you in. Don't bring misfortune into my house, go away.'

The doctor's assistant closed the door in the girl's face.

Renate stood there for a few moments, as if waiting for someone or something, then turned and went uncertainly down the street, not knowing where to go now.

Suddenly, the door to the doctor's assistant's house opened again. Anelė ran out, her face streaked with tears. When she caught up with Renate, she thrust a bundle of food into her hands, hurriedly made the sign of the cross over her and ran back to the house and closed the door.

Renate carried on walking along the road.

RENATE WAS SITTING down, leaning against an old bath-house and watching the spring birds as they chirped in the swaying trees.

The sun was shining, the brooks babbling, grass sprouting from the earth.

Renate untied the bundle the doctor's assistant had given her – in it was a piece of ham, a slice of bread and two eggs. She began to eat.

RENATE ENTERED AN empty, echoing church. It was the same church she'd been in with Stasė.

She looked up at the statues, at Jesus Christ hanging on the cross.

She heard a cough – a man came out of the sacristy, knelt down briefly as he passed the altar and looked at her word-lessly. It was the exterminators' driver; he had been there when they took Antanas and Stasė away, but had stood apart from the rest.

Renate went into the sacristy.

The priest, dressed in his cassock, was arranging his litur-gical garments.

Renate entered noiselessly and watched him as he worked.

As if he'd sensed something, the priest turned around. He looked surprised to see Renate. He smiled.

'Ah, it's our Marytė.'

'They took my Mama Stasė away.'

'I know. Stasė and Antanas are fine people. May the Lord help them in their journey of sorrow and on their path of suffering.'

'Help me, I beg you, take me in, I beg you! I believe in God – I'm a Catholic.'

The priest looked at Renate. His expression seemed grave, but perhaps he was simply lost in thought.

Renate was eating soup out of a large bowl.

She could hear the priest talking to his housekeeper.

The priest gave the housekeeper a piece of paper.

'Take the girl to this address. There are still some nuns

there, who'll look after her. As it happens, Boleslavas is going to be taking the exterminators to Kaunas – don't tell him who she is, just let him hand her over to Father Ramojus – I went to university with him, he'll know what to do. The nuns will take her and look after her. Kaunas is a large town, it'll be safer for her there.'

The spring sun was shining brightly. Boleslavas, the driver, held Renate by the hand. They went over to the lorry. Several exterminators were waiting with rifles slung over their shoulders.

They were smoking roll-ups, joking among themselves. Boleslavas greeted them.

'And who's this, your daughter?' asked one of the exterminators.

'No, a relative, I have to take her to Kaunas. Can you make room for her?'

'We can,' nodded the exterminator.

At that moment, Mikita appeared from behind the lorry. Mikita's eyes met hers. Renate was so scared she couldn't speak. All the exterminators were waiting to hear her name. Renate was silent. But Mikita smiled.

'Her name's Marytė, I know her. Let's get in, lift her up and put her in the trailer. The lieutenant is coming,' said Mikita.

The exterminators took hold of Renate and lifted her in.

The lieutenant came up, gave the exterminators a stern glance and sat down next to the driver.

The men climbed in and the lorry moved off.

THE EXTERMINATORS' LORRY left the town. The cold spring wind pierced right through their greatcoats; they put their collars up and pulled down the ear flaps of their caps. They were sitting on the planks that ran along the sides of the trailer, holding their rifles tightly, the butts resting on the floor. Some of them, the smarter ones, had got in first and were huddled together in the trailer, in the straw – it was warmer that way. Mikita told Renate to make herself comfortable among the half-sitting, half-lying men. Once she'd squeezed in between them, the wind hardly reached her; she was protected by the cabin and the broad-shouldered exterminators. The girl could only see the clouds, the sky and the branches of the town's trees, which were now disappearing behind her, and the faces of the armed men, red from the wind, who hadn't found room to lie down on the floor. Renate looked at them and surprised herself when she realised that they were all much the same as anyone else.

The lorry was soon travelling through the flat countryside far beyond the town. Looking up, all you could see were the clouds falling on top of one another, forming large plumes like smoke from a never-ending war. Renate found the sky unsettling, and her heart filled with darkness and an incomprehensible fear. She was thinking about her mother and Auntie Lotte, she remembered Monika, Brigitte, Heinz, Auntie Martha, she remembered everyone who had been good to her, as well as those who had done her harm. At times the lorry shook the passengers, at times it rocked them like a baby in a cradle, but all that movement merged into the rhythmic, sleep-inducing motif of an endless music.

The girl's eyes began to close, the anxiety and fatigue of the last couple of days lay on her eyelids like a heavy, almost unbearable burden. To the whirring sound of the engine, the rattle of the wheels and the whistling of the wind, Renate slowly slipped into a dream, reality merged with a fairy tale. She saw her mother, but couldn't make out her face. Her mother had turned away and for some reason didn't want to turn back, to look at Renate, her beloved daughter. Renate wanted to call out, but her voice was trapped in her throat. And when she finally managed, with great difficulty, to utter her mother's name, when her mother finally turned around, she saw it wasn't her mother at all. The woman still resembled her mother, but her face was different; it looked exactly like that of the Russian woman who had moved into their house. In her arms was the fat, spoilt cat.

The first shot woke Renate from her slumber. The lorry was in the forest now. The men quickly grabbed hold of their guns and squatted down to hide behind the trailer's sides. The sound of automatic weapons rang out and the exterminators returned fire. A shot of red sprayed out from the head of one of the men, the youngest one – he fell over the side and lay in the road. The lorry shook violently, lurched and slammed into the stump of a tree at the roadside. Renate hit her head against the back of the cabin. The world started spinning, something fell on top of her and everything seemed far away, faded to an echo, as if she had fallen into a well.

When she regained consciousness, all was still.

Someone was lying across her, pressing down on her and preventing her from breathing, but nothing really seemed to hurt – perhaps only the top of her head – though she had the salty taste of blood in her mouth.

The girl tried to move, somehow managing to free her

arm, which had gone numb. Summoning all her strength, she pushed away the body lying on top of her and crawled out from underneath it. It was already twilight, and darkness was falling fast. Everything seemed to have happened so quickly. Several men were lying in the lorry, all of them dead. The one who had fallen on top of Renate turned out to be Mikita. She stood up and saw that the other men were also dead, lying in the road or on the verge in strange poses. She had encountered death more than once during this horrific year, but this time it seemed even more terrible – perhaps because the treetops were rustling as if the wind was also guilty. Her legs shaking, Renate climbed over the side of the trailer onto a small ladder and jumped down. She walked around the lorry and saw the driver Boleslavas hanging out of the cabin. He must have opened the door in an attempt to run away. Renate wiped her lips with her hand, and saw red on her palm. But she wasn't in any pain, so where had that blood come from? The girl realised then that it wasn't her blood, but Mikita's. It seemed strange to Renate that her blood could taste the same as someone else's, but she still felt nauseous. She sat down in a ditch until the queasiness had passed, then washed her hands and face in the melting snow. The cold water refreshed her. Renate got up and began walking down the middle of the road. She climbed over a fir tree that had been felled by the partisans and carried on, not once looking back.

Renate soon came to the edge of the forest; either it was not very large, or the partisans had placed the ambush just ahead of where the exterminators were due to emerge from the trees. The day was drawing to a close. The world was flooded with the evening blue, and a mist was rising at the forest edge. Renate kept walking on, not knowing where she should go or what she would find in the distance.

She heard the sound of an engine, and ran to the side of the road, dived behind some bushes and waited. A motorcycle and some sort of a saloon, black and shiny, appeared. Renate imagined that the driver was death itself, come to see if those who had been killed were really dead, to see if there was even just a breath of life left in them. Death had come to collect the corpses. Renate couldn't stay there, she couldn't keep going down this road – she ran off, straight into the mist, through a sodden spring meadow, as far away from it as possible.

Dawn arrived at last. The mist and everything around was suffused with the early-morning light. Renate had found an old haystack the night before, and was snuggled into it. An animal, perhaps a fox or badger, had created a burrow in the bottom of the haystack, which she had made into a burrow of her own.

A frost had come during the night. Although Renate had been lucky to find such a good hiding place while lost on a spring evening, she was still very cold. Her feet felt like they were made of wood, and she was afraid to move, to risk dissipating the little warmth she felt and to return to that terrible, shaking cold. Renate's eyes began to close and she dozed off again; and so she slept all night, only waking up occasionally before falling once more into a dense, cold dream. In the dream, she could see the dogs and Heinz, she could see Boris, but she couldn't see her mother. She cried and begged her mother to show herself. Everyone else had appeared, but not her mother. She then dreamt about Stasė. For some reason, Stasė was sitting on a pile of firewood and singing – sadly, forlornly, the same song that Renate's mother had so loved to sing. Renate wanted to dance, but she couldn't move her body, it was heavy as a log and her legs wouldn't obey her, and she began to weep from helplessness.

Finally, the morning conquered the night and Renate awoke once more. Somewhere in the distance jays were shrieking. The girl climbed out of the haystack and now saw that there was a farmstead just a hundred metres away, but it looked like it had been burnt down several months ago, all the buildings, everything – all that was left was the chimney sticking up into the sky. The chimney and a pile of old hay, nothing more. How strange that the hay hadn't burnt, thought Renate.

The girl was deathly cold and stiff. She tried to warm up, to move her numbed legs, but her head started to spin.

Renate understood only one thing – she had to keep going. And so she set off.

A small figure in those endless fields.

Renate walked for a long time, swaying from side to side. She began to count her steps, to recite the only prayer she knew: 'Our Father, who art in heaven...'

Then the clouds unexpectedly parted, and the sun shone down on her like a golden hammer being brought down to strike the earth, filling the air with sounds; Renate could hear the birds singing. It was as if the sheet of night had been torn apart, and the cold pushed away.

Renate walked along to the sound of a lark singing as it hovered in the sky.

She was no longer cold. Yesterday's journey in the exterminators' lorry now seemed like a dream. The corpses of the men – a fragment from a fairy tale she had once heard.

Renate suddenly realised that she hadn't seen the sun for such a long time she'd forgotten that it had ever shone. Her small world had been filled only with the clouds, the mists and the snow. But now something had changed.

Then, as if out of nowhere, as if out of the remnants of the mist, out of the void, a small horse appeared. It shook its large head, its mane long and yellow, a star on its forehead. The horse was pulling a cart, the wheels creaking and turning at great speed.

'My child, where are you going on your own, so early in the morning?' the woman in the cart asked Renate with a smile.

'My name is Marytė,' answered the girl in Lithuanian.

The man holding the reins gave a thunderous laugh, showing his white, even teeth. 'It's nice that your name is Marytė, but where are you going?'

'I'm a Catholic,' said Renate, as Marytė.

'Hallelujah,' said the woman, still smiling. 'We're also Catholics, we're on our way to church.'

Renate said nothing, just stared at them with expressionless eyes.

'We have to go to church today, Christ rose again on this day.'

'Get in the cart,' said the man.

'Where's your mother?' asked the woman.

'In Kaunas,' replied Marytė.

The kind people didn't ask her any more questions, accustomed as they were to all sorts of travellers, people who had found their way here from other parts – it was just the times they lived in. So many orphans were wandering from village to village, from town to town: Russian and German children, and Lithuanians too. The woman rummaged in her linen bag, took out a cake wrapped in a kerchief and offered a large slice to the girl, without even asking if she was hungry. The cake had cottage cheese and cinnamon in it – it looked and smelt so delicious.

Marytė was travelling along through the shining spring fields, drawn by the merry little horse, with its bright tail swishing from side to side. The sun was warming the ground and the mist had disappeared. The sun was warming the girl too, and she began to nod off, her eyes closing, as if her eyelids were too heavy.

The woman said, 'Lie down for a bit on the straw, Marytė, I can see your eyes are closing.'

Marytė lay down on the golden straw. The woman covered her legs with a horse blanket and Marytė felt very comfortable. The man cracked his whip and the little horse hurried on at quite a pace. At last, the girl felt truly calm inside, and she fell asleep.

'The girl's probably ill,' said the woman to her husband. 'You can see she hasn't had enough sleep.'

Marytė dreamt of a huge meadow, where cakes sprouted out of the earth like mushrooms—

'Whoa,' the man shouted. The horse stopped and Renate woke up.

The sun had already travelled far across the sky, and the cart had reached the outskirts of the town.

Renate watched as the couple changed their shoes; you have to go to church in your Sunday best. They hid their everyday shoes under the straw.

They travelled on. The woman smiled at the girl and took a red egg out of her basket; it was an Easter egg, decorated with crosses and lines.

'Take it,' said the woman. 'You can take it into the church, the priest will bless it and you'll have a blessed Easter egg.'

'Thank you,' said Renate.

They drove on; the church was still a little way down the road. People were streaming though the churchyard gates; several carts had been left outside and the horses, tied up, were snorting and neighing as they pawed at the earth. Mothers led their children by the hand, and the men took off their caps as they walked through the gates.

The man who had brought Marytė tied his horse up not far from the churchyard wall.

The woman waited for him, adjusted her scarf, took a handkerchief from her handbag and tucked it into her sleeve.

Renate was holding the Easter egg in her hand, unsure what to do next. She would have liked to go with the couple, she would have liked to ask if she could stay with them, she would be good to them, she would do whatever work she was given, she wouldn't be a burden. But the woman said goodbye and the man winked at her, a merry, even mischievous wink – *Stay well, my child*, the wink said. And before Renate could say anything, the couple joined the stream of people hurrying into the church.

The girl went over to the churchyard wall. When she was sure that the couple could no longer see her, she greedily ate the egg and threw the red eggshell on the ground.

She walked along the wall and stopped by the side gates.

The church bells began to ring overhead and birds flew up into the sky.

The door opened wide and a solemn procession appeared.

Renate was entranced by the girls' white dresses, by the priests walking under the canopy, by the statue of the Virgin Mary carried by the clerics, and by the singing women.

She found it all so beautiful, but didn't dare go any closer. She was sad, and sorry that she had eaten the Easter egg.

RENATE WAS TREMBLING from the cold, even though the sun was so warm and spring seemed to be emerging from the pot in which it had been trapped by winter. The girl walked along the churchyard wall and noticed the beggars sitting by the gates and lining the paths leading to the church. Renate's head began to spin, and she sat down on a huge stone. She sat and watched the birds picking at their feathers in the warmth of the sun. She felt weighed down by a heavy fatigue, and the world appeared to her as if through a mist. Renate didn't want to fall asleep, so she went to look for the cart of the couple who had brought her here, but couldn't find it. She walked and walked, circling the church, and thought she recognised the spot under some tall linden trees where the little horse with the light-coloured mane had been tied up, but there were too many carts, and she couldn't see the horse. The girl waited, but it soon became clear that she wouldn't find them, those good people with whom she wanted to stay.

The day was passing; people streamed out of the church on their own or in groups. The horses, drowsy in the heat, began to snort and neigh again as the men called to them. The carts set off towards home, full of smiling, joyful people dressed in their Sunday best, each taking away with them the girl's hope that she would ever meet the kind couple again.

The churchyard emptied; even the beggars went off to wherever they had come from. Pieces of straw were blowing through the air on the wind, jackdaws were cawing as they searched through the horse dung.

Renate was left on her own. She felt sad and lonely, and would have liked to cry, but instead she felt herself breaking out in a sweat.

The girl sat down on another sun-warmed stone, untied her headscarf and felt the wind touch her hair. She closed her eyes and sat there, almost asleep.

Renate couldn't say how much time had passed, but eventually, at the sound of voices, she raised her head again. A family was walking past – an elegant gentleman in a hat and light-coloured jacket, and a slender, tall woman with curly blonde hair decorated with a headband with small artificial flowers. *What a very beautiful woman*, thought Renate.

The woman was holding a small boy by the hand. The boy pointed at Renate and they exchanged a few words. It seemed like the man was gently scolding the boy. Then they stopped, and the boy ran up to Renate and held out an Easter egg.

'Please take it,' said the child. 'It's a blessed egg.'

The girl took the gift from the boy, who skipped off to his family, to his mama and papa.

Renate stared at the Easter egg in her hand in disbelief – it was the same red as the one she'd so carelessly eaten, decorated with the same little crosses and lines. *It must be the same one, the same egg.* The girl's heart began to pound with emotion. She would have liked to say something to those people, but they had disappeared. All that was left was the sun, the dust and the birds.

RENATE WAS WANDERING aimlessly along the streets of an unfamiliar town. Cheerful noises were coming through the open windows of many of the houses: people were celebrating this miraculous Sunday, apparently paying no mind to the postwar shortages or the new occupation, of which the girl knew nothing at all. The sun grew redder, its rays cooler. The evening was advancing ever more quickly, and the chilly wind was a reminder of winter.

Renate found a ruined house with most of its roof destroyed, and curled up on some planks of wood in the farthest corner.

Night fell, dark and cold.

Dogs barked somewhere close by in the street, followed by shouts. The girl was afraid. She cowered in the corner, she was cold, she was trembling, but it was still better here than outside; at least the wind couldn't reach her. She was holding the Easter egg with both hands, and it seemed to warm her a little. Renate was hungry, but she didn't have the slightest intention of eating that red egg. The endless night brought memories with it – she was walking through the forest again, saw some soldiers beating Auntie Lotte, then Antanas was there with his one arm chopping firewood, and she was giving him the wood to be chopped.

It was early morning when Renate left the ruined house. She looked around the street and started walking, with no destination in mind. Her legs were heavy, her eyelids even heavier, but she walked and walked through the town, which was beginning to wake up. She gradually started to warm up a little in the bright sunshine, but she had a fever, her head was spinning and sweat was pouring down her face.

Suddenly she heard beautiful music, and she thought that she was still dreaming. Someone was playing Erik Satie's *Gnossienne* No. 5, but it didn't sound the same as when her mother had played it. This person was pressing down on the keys much harder, as if trying to chop them up. Renate was gripped by fear as she approached the sound.

The music grew louder.

Finally, Renate found the place where the music was coming from. She was standing in an empty street by a damaged wall, and saw a house in front of her, its windows open to the spring and the sun. Behind the windows, in a brightly lit room, girls were dancing – little ballerinas. Renate saw the piano, a thick-set woman sitting at it, and next to her an elegant, tall woman with a headband in her hair.

Renate stared into this miraculous world, unable to tear her eyes away.

The dance ended, the girls cheered and started asking the woman, who was their dance teacher, for something. She laughed, seeming to agree to the request. Then, all of a sudden, the ballerinas spilled out into the street, holding eggs painted in various colours, and a trough for rolling the eggs.

The teacher and the thick-set, whiskered accompanist went with them, carrying some Easter eggs of their own.

The girls laughed as they started rolling the eggs.

Renate's eyes filled with tears. They stung. Her cheeks became wet with tears – or perhaps it was sweat – and she was shivering violently. She took one step forward, then another one, and took the coloured egg the little boy had given her from her pocket. She held it out to that very beautiful woman, the little ballerinas' teacher, who, to Renate, suddenly looked very much like Stasė.

The woman saw Renate and the world seemed to slow down, almost coming to a complete halt. The girl understood that she might not have enough time, that she had to say something quickly; she held out her red Easter egg to the beautiful woman, who came over to her, bent down, smiled and asked her something.

'My name is Marytė,' said Renate, and the woman took the blessed egg from the girl's hand.

Marytė fell into a deep, black well, but felt no fear.

The woman wasn't able to catch the girl in time, as she lost consciousness and fell onto the dusty street.

The little ballerinas flocked around her, frightened: 'Is she dead? Is she dead?'

'No, she's alive,' said their teacher. She lifted Renate up and carried her into the house.

The accompanist and the little ballerinas followed them inside.

A Note from the Author

You could say that the subject of this book found me. The film director Jonas Marcinkevičius, who is no longer with us, suggested in around 1996 that we should make a documentary about the German children who had gone to Lithuania after the Second World War in an attempt to survive. It was then that I heard the German word *Wolfskinder*, 'wolf-children', for the first time. It wasn't surprising that no one knew of the suffering those children had endured; even the Germans themselves knew very little about it. Here's an example: much later, in 2009 or so, I made the acquaintance of some young Germans. We were talking about various things, in particular about writing. I mentioned to them that I was writing about the wolf-children. 'Is that a story about Tarzan?' one of those educated people asked me, in all seriousness. That question only reinforced my thinking that it was necessary to speak and write about the subject.

The idea Jonas and I had sadly came to nothing, because our application for funding failed to convince the relevant ministry, and we did not receive the necessary grant. A long time later, my friend Rolandas Skaisgirys, a producer, unexpectedly asked me if I knew anything about the German children who had come to Lithuania after the war to beg for bread and a place to stay – the wolf-children. I was amazed. It turns out that Ričardas Savickas, a businessman, whose mother had herself been one of these wolf-children, had found Rolandas. Ričardas wanted this subject not to be forgotten, wanted the misfortunes those people had suffered to be remembered. He spoke about the life of his mother, Renata Markewitz-Savickienė, and many of the details of that story have found their way into this book.

Some time later, when we announced that we had decided to make a film about the wolf-children, I began getting phone calls and letters, both from people I knew and from strangers. They told me about their neighbours, or friends of friends, who had been wolf-children, or who knew something about those postwar years. Around that time, I got to know a woman who had also come to Lithuania after the war to look for a way to survive. Her first name was unusually similar to Ričardas's mother's first name – it differed in only one letter. Her first name was Renate. Renate told me about her experiences in the postwar years, about the people who had given her shelter. I found out many of the exact details surrounding those events, which may seem of little importance, but are in fact very important, in order to convey a sense of the horror and dreadful despair of those days. It seemed to me that while she was telling her story I could see, hear and feel the living people involved. It was then that I understood how I should write the story.

Is more of Renata or Renate to be found in the small girl, lost among the snowdrifts and people, about whom you've just read? I don't know.

Unfortunately I am unable to reveal the surname of the second woman, because after the book was written and I tried to meet with her again to talk about the present and to use that interview for an epilogue, Renate suddenly refused, saying that she no longer wished to remember anything, to comment on anything, to relate anything: 'Everything has long been dead to me.' With those words, she put down the receiver.

All I can say now is that Renate lives in Lithuania, worked as a teacher all her adult life and is now retired. She is not in contact with the other wolf-children, and although she found her relatives in Germany, they have sadly not remained in touch.

Alvydas Šlepikas

Oneworld, Many Voices

Bringing you exceptional writing
from around the world

The Unit by Ninni Holmqvist (Swedish)
Translated by Marlaine Delargy

Twice Born by Margaret Mazzantini (Italian)
Translated by Ann Gagliardi

Things We Left Unsaid by Zoya Pirzad (Persian)
Translated by Franklin Lewis

The Space Between Us by Zoya Pirzad (Persian)
Translated by Amy Motlagh

The Hen Who Dreamed She Could Fly by Sun-mi Hwang
(Korean) Translated by Chi-Young Kim

The Hilltop by Assaf Gavron (Hebrew)
Translated by Steven Cohen

Morning Sea by Margaret Mazzantini (Italian)
Translated by Ann Gagliardi

A Perfect Crime by A Yi (Chinese)
Translated by Anna Holmwood

The Meursault Investigation by Kamel Daoud (French)
Translated by John Cullen

Minus Me by Ingelin Røssland (YA) (Norwegian)
Translated by Deborah Dawkin

Laurus by Eugene Vodolazkin (Russian)
Translated by Lisa C. Hayden

Masha Regina by Vadim Levental (Russian)
Translated by Lisa C. Hayden

French Concession by Xiao Bai (Chinese)
Translated by Chenxin Jiang

The Sky Over Lima by Juan Gómez Bárcena (Spanish)
Translated by Andrea Rosenberg

A Very Special Year by Thomas Montasser (German)
Translated by Jamie Bulloch

Umami by Laia Jufresa (Spanish)
Translated by Sophie Hughes

The Hermit by Thomas Rydahl (Danish)
Translated by K. E. Semmel

The Peculiar Life of a Lonely Postman by Denis Thériault
(French) Translated by Liedewy Hawke

Three Envelopes by Nir Hezroni (Hebrew)
Translated by Steven Cohen

Fever Dream by Samanta Schweblin (Spanish)
Translated by Megan McDowell

The Postman's Fiancée by Denis Thériault (French)
Translated by John Cullen

The Invisible Life of Euridice Gusmao by Martha Batalha
(Brazilian Portuguese) Translated by Eric M. B. Becker

The Temptation to Be Happy by Lorenzo Marone
(Italian) Translated by Shaun Whiteside

Sweet Bean Paste by Durian Sukegawa (Japanese)
Translated by Alison Watts

They Know Not What They Do by Jussi Valtonen (Finnish)
Translated by Kristian London

The Tiger and the Acrobat by Susanna Tamaro (Italian)
Translated by Nicoleugenia Prezzavento and Vicki Satlow

The Woman at 1,000 Degrees by Hallgrímur Helgason
(Icelandic) Translated by Brian FitzGibbon

Frankenstein in Baghdad by Ahmed Saadawi (Arabic)
Translated by Jonathan Wright

Back Up by Paul Colize (French)
Translated by Louise Rogers Lalaurie

Damnation by Peter Beck (German)
Translated by Jamie Bulloch

Oneiron by Laura Lindstedt (Finnish)
Translated by Owen F. Witesman

The Boy Who Belonged to the Sea by Denis Thériault
(French) Translated by Liedewy Hawke

The Baghdad Clock by Shahad Al Rawi (Arabic)
Translated by Luke Leafgren

The Aviator by Eugene Vodolazkin (Russian)
Translated by Lisa C. Hayden

Lala by Jacek Dehnel (Polish)
Translated by Antonia Lloyd-Jones

Bogotá 39: New Voices from Latin America
(Spanish and Portuguese) Short story anthology

Last Instructions by Nir Hezroni (Hebrew)
Translated by Steven Cohen

The Day I Found You by Pedro Chagas Freitas (Portuguese)
Translated by Daniel Hahn

Solovyov and Larionov by Eugene Vodolazkin (Russian)
Translated by Lisa C. Hayden

In/Half by Jasmin B. Frelih (Slovenian)
Translated by Jason Blake

Alvydas Šlepikas is one of Lithuania's most renowned contemporary writers. He is a poet, prose writer, playwright, screenwriter, actor and director. He has edited publications produced by the Lithuanian Spring Poetry Festival as well as the cultural weekly *Literatūra ir menas*, where he is currently fiction editor. *In the Shadow of Wolves*, which was named Book of the Year in Lithuania in 2012, is his first novel.

Romas Kinka works as a forensic linguist and a literary translator. Born in Lithuania, he has lived in England on and off since the age of six but returns to his homeland every day by translating the work of Lithuanian authors.